FAITH LARGE PRINT

Amish Romance

RUTH HARTZLER

Faith LARGE PRINT
(The Amish Buggy Horse Book 1)
Ruth Hartzler

ISBN 9781925689259

This is a work of fiction. Any resemblance to any person, living or dead, is purely coincidental. The personal names have been invented by the author, and any likeness to the name of any person, living or dead, is purely coincidental.

Glossary

Pennsylvania Dutch is a dialect. It is often written as it sounds, which is why you will see the same word written several different ways. The word 'Dutch' has nothing to do with Holland, but rather is likely a corruption of the German word 'Deitsch' or 'Deutsch'.

Glossary

ab im kopp - addled in the head

Ach! (also, *Ack!*) - Oh!

aenti - aunt

appeditlich - delicious

Ausbund - Amish hymn book

bedauerlich - sad

bloobier - blueberry

boppli - baby

bopplin - babies

bro - bread

bruder(s) - brother(s)

bu - boy

Budget, The - weekly newspaper for Amish and Mennonite communities. Based on Sugarcreek, Ohio, and has 2 versions, Local and National.

buwe - boys

daag - day

Daed, *Datt*, *Dat* (vocative) - Dad

Diary, The - Lancaster County based Amish newspaper. Focus is on Old Order Amish.

Dawdi (also, *Daadi*) (vocative) - Grandfather

dawdi haus (also, *daadi haus*, *grossdawdi haus*) - grandfather's or grandparents' house (often a small house behind the main house)

de Bo - boyfriend

Die Botschaft - Amish weekly newspaper. Based in PA but its focus is nation-wide.

demut - humility

denki (or *danki*) - thank you

Der Herr - The Lord

dochder - daughter

dokter - doctor

doplich - clumsy

dumm - dumb

dummkopf - idiot, dummy

Dutch Blitz - Amish card game

English (or *Englisch*) (adjective) - A non-Amish person

Englischer (noun) - A non-Amish person

familye - family

ferhoodled - foolish, crazy

fraa - wife, woman

froh - happy

freind - friend

freinden - friends

gegisch - silly

geh - go

gern gheschen (also, gern *gschehne*) - you're welcome

Gott (also, *Gotte*) - God

grank - sick, ill

grossboppli - grandbaby

grossdawdi (also, *dawdi, daadi haus*, *gross dawdi)* - grandfather, or, in some communities, great grandfather

grosskinskind - great-grandchild

grosskinskinner - great-grandchildren

grossmammi (or *grossmudder*) - grandmother

gross-sohn - grandson

grossvadder - grandfather (see also *grossdawdi*)

gude mariye - good morning

guten nacht (also, *gut nacht*) - good night

gude nochmiddaag - good afternoon

gut - good

haus - house

Herr - Mr.

Hiya - Hi

hochmut - pride

Hullo (also, *Hallo*) - Hello

hungerich - hungry

Ich liebe dich - I love you

jah (also *ya*) - yes

kaffi (also, *kaffee*) - coffee

kapp - prayer covering worn by women

kichli - cookie

kichlin - cookies

kinn (also, *kind*) - child

kinner - children

kinskinner - Grandchildren

Kumme (or *Kumm*) - Come

lieb - love, sweetheart

liewe - a term of endearment, dear, love

liede - song

maid (also, *maed*) - girls

maidel (also, *maedel*) - girl

Mamm (also, *Mammi*) - Mother, Mom

Mammi - Grandmother

mann - man

mariye-esse - breakfast

mei - my

meidung - shunning

mei lieb - my love

mein liewe - my dear, my love

menner - men

mudder - mother

naerfich - nervous

naut (also, *nacht*) - night

nee (also *nein*) - no

nix - nothing

nohma - name

onkel - uncle

Ordnung - "Order", the unwritten Amish set of rules, different in each community

piffle (also, *piddle*) - to waste time or kill time

Plain - referring to the Amish way of life

rett (also, *redd*) - to put (items) away or to clean up.

rootsh (also, *ruch*) - not being able to sit still.

rumspringa (also, *rumschpringe*) - Running around years - when Amish youth (usually around the age of sixteen) leave the community for time and can be English, and decide whether to commit to the Amish way of life and be baptized.

schatzi - honey

schee - pretty, handsome

schecklich - scary

schmaert - smart

schtupp - family room

schweschder - sister

schweschdern - sisters

schwoger - brother-in-law

seltsam - strange, unnatural

sohn - son

vadder - father

verboten - forbidden

Vorsinger - Song leader

was its let - what is the matter?

wie gehts - how are you?

wilkum (also, *wilkom*) - welcome

wunderbar (also, *wunderbaar*) - wonderful

yer - you

yourself - yourself

youngie (also, *young)* - the youth

yung - young

Chapter One

Nettie sat staring at the cards sent from all over the country by people she did not even know existed. She was grateful that the bishop and his wife had taken over the funeral and arranged everything, despite the fact that she had not seen them for many years.

Nettie had noticed the curious glances sent her way throughout the viewing and the funeral, but she had been too shocked to care at the time. Now, the full impact of her *mudder's* passing had come home to roost.

Nettie's invalid *mudder*, Elma, had not wanted any involvement with the community, more so as the years had passed. Nettie was virtually a prisoner in the home, only venturing out once a month for food and any necessities. Even then, she had to be back by the expected time, or be subject to another of her mother's tantrums.

Elma had been a demanding, controlling woman prone to frequent outbursts of temper. Nettie was her only child, and had been her sole caregiver. Elma had even refused to let the bishop visit in recent years, and had not attended church meetings for the same length of time. As a result, Nettie knew no one in the community, at least no one that she could remember.

Although their *haus* was at the end of a lane, the other end of the lane intersected a road that led to an *Englischer* school, and some of the local school children often taunted Nettie as she drove past.

Nettie's buggy horse, Harry, had been her only companion, and she used to put her face in his mane and tell him all her troubles. Yet, the week before Elma died, Harry had gone lame, and the veterinarian had said he was old and had to be retired permanently. Nettie was grateful that her *mudder* had allowed her to summon a veterinarian to the farm; no other *Englischers*, let alone Amish, had visited the *haus* in the several years before Elma had died.

Nettie looked around her at the food that the community had brought her. "That will keep me going until I can buy another buggy horse," she said aloud. Nettie was accustomed to speaking aloud to herself, as Elma had been deaf, and Nettie had to yell to make herself heard. It was good to speak in a normal voice, even if only to herself.

Nettie sunk to the floor and crouched there with her head in her hands. Even when she had felt trapped in the *haus*, she had still been able to escape to the stores once a month.

Now, even that option was taken away from her. "At least I'll have the money to buy a buggy horse soon," Nettie said, to no one in particular. "Then I'll be able to go out whenever I like."

The thought roused Nettie from her self pity. She got up and walked through the *haus*, drawing aside curtains and opening windows. Her *mudder*, Elma, had liked the curtains tightly drawn at all times, and the windows shut. It had always been dark and dim inside, even on the brightest, sunny day. Since Elma had gone to be with *Gott*, Nettie had kept every window in the *haus* open, letting in the fresh air to drive out the mustiness, dust, and gloom of decades. Nevertheless, the unpleasant, musty smell still lingered to some degree.

Nettie walked into her favorite room, the one she used for sewing and mending, as well as drying. There were two sewing machines, hers and her *mudder's*, although that one had not been used for years. It was covered with pots of herbs, as Nettie started her herbs in there. Her *mudder* had not objected to that, for it was from her *mudder* that Nettie got her training about herbs and their medicinal uses. Yet, the crocheted doilies which covered every available space were also her *mudder's*. Nettie regarded them with horror. They were aged and yellowing, and smelled of decay. She made a mental note to throw them in the trash, but right now, she was too overwhelmed with everything to do anything other than her usual chores.

Nettie returned to the kitchen to pour herself a mug of *kaffi*. Elma had always objected to the smell of *kaffi* and yelled at Nettie every morning, but Nettie's one pleasure in life had been her morning *kaffi*. Nettie considered that the place seemed empty without her *mudder*. As much as Nettie loved and missed her *mudder*, she had been nothing less than a tyrant. In fact, Elma had made Nettie's life hell. Just thinking the word *hell* made Nettie guilty, and her hand flew to her mouth. She sat down on an old, wooden chair in the kitchen, but in a moment of rebellion, put her feet up on the table. The thought of what Elma would have done if she could see Nettie now, set Nettie off into a fit of giggles, and then laughter which bordered on the hysterical. *I wonder if I am mad*, Nettie thought, *like the Englisch kinner say I am*.

Chapter Two

Nettie's heart leaped to her mouth when she heard the knock on the door. Who could it be? Her *mudder* had always insisted that she hide if anyone knocked, and so the door was never answered. Nettie took a deep breath and forced herself over to the door. Perhaps it was just the bishop.

Nettie opened the door to find an old, stooped *Englischer* man standing on the doorstep. He smelled strongly of mothballs, and at once Nettie felt sick to the stomach.

The old man wasted no time introducing himself. "Good morning, Miss Swarey. My name is William Koble. I'm your mother's lawyer. You wrote to me when your mother died. Please accept my condolences."

Nettie stood there staring at the man. She had found his name and address, along with the word, 'lawyer,' scrawled on a piece of paper when going through her *mudder's* things, and, as he was the only lawyer mentioned, she had written to him about the will. After a moment, Nettie collected her thoughts. "Oh yes, Mr. Koble, please come in." She showed the lawyer into the living room, and then hurried to shut the windows after he sneezed violently three times in a row.

Mr. Koble sat down in the deep sofa, and Nettie wondered if he would be able to get out of it unaided. "Would you like a cup of hot tea? Or a glass of water?"

"Yes, please."

Nettie frowned, not knowing which of the two he wanted, but did not like to ask again, so soon returned with both a glass of water and a cup of hot tea, which she placed beside Mr. Koble on a musty, yellowing doily on top of a small, round table. Nettie also offered him some pumpkin whoopie pies, which he refused.

"Now, down to business, Miss Swarey." His voice was frail.

Nettie sat in her *mudder's* old rocker recliner opposite him, and nodded expectantly.

"I would have called, of course, but you have no phone."

Nettie felt a twinge of guilt for making the elderly man drive out all the way to see her, but she had no choice. She did not have a phone, and that's all there was to it. He would have known that when he took on an Amish client.

After another sneeze, Mr. Koble spoke. "You said in your letter that you found my name and address written on a piece of paper with your mother's things?"

Nettie nodded again.

"And there was no copy of a Will and Testament?"

Nettie grew alarmed. "*Nee*, does that matter? Do you have the will?"

Mr. Koble was quick to reassure her. "Oh yes, there's no worry on that account. We do have a legal Last Will and Testament of your mother's. The only thing is, it was signed many years ago and we have not heard from your mother since, so it is possible that there is a later Will and Testament."

Nettie bit her lip. "What will happen if there is?"

"Well, the later Will and Testament will obviously take precedence in that case, of course." Mr. Koble peered at Nettie over the top of his glasses, and she felt silly for asking the question. "You have no record of any other lawyers?" he asked. "If so, perhaps you could write to them and ask."

Nettie shook her head. "*Nee*, you were the only one I could find any mention of."

Mr. Koble peered at Nettie once more, and then said, "I see. Well, I shall read you the Will and Testament, if I may."

Nettie leaned back in the rocker recliner as Mr. Koble slowly read the Will and Testament to her. It seemed like a lot of legal terminology without coming to any real point. Nettie had spent a sleepless night, as she had been used to getting up every few hours to attend to her *mudder*, and now that she no longer had to, her sleep patterns had become even more disturbed. She felt herself drifting off to sleep.

Nettie was startled back to wakefulness when Mr. Koble's voice grew louder. "I'm sorry, did you say *cats*?"

"Yes, Miss Swarey, I'm sorry to say that I did." His tone sounded entirely regretful.

"Cats?" Nettie shook herself and tried to wake up fully. What would cats have to do with anything? Perhaps she dreamed it.

Mr. Koble was still talking. "Yes, as the Will and Testament states, the house and land are now fully yours, or will be after probate, as will be all the furniture and all the goods and chattels within the entire property, including the buggy, the harness, and any buggy horses, and all livestock."

Nettie was not at all surprised—that was precisely as she had expected. Her *vadder* had died many years ago when she was a newborn *boppli*, and she was the only child. There were no relatives, not as far as she knew.

"And as I just said," Mr. Koble continued, his voice now again shaky, "your mother was a wealthy woman."

"Wealthy?" Nettie could not help but interrupt. Sure, they had never wanted for anything, and neither she nor her *mudder* worked. Nettie knew that her *mudder* had savings from when the alfalfa farm was worked, back before Nettie's *vadder* died, but she had no idea that her *mudder* was actually wealthy. Nettie milked the goat, and grew all their own vegetables. As her *mudder's* teeth were bad, they very rarely ate meat, so they were all but self sufficient. There was plenty of grazing for the buggy horse, Harry, and he had never needed grain to maintain his fat, shiny condition.

Mr. Koble simply shrugged. "This is rich alfalfa farming land, Miss Swarey. Now, I'm not sure if you heard me before, or perhaps you are in some kind of shock, which is entirely understandable. However, I must repeat, your mother left you the farm and house in its entirety, but every last cent she left to the Sunnybanks Stray Cat Protection League."

Chapter Three

Nettie grasped at her own throat with both hands. "Is this a joke?" she asked. "Cats? But *Mamm* didn't even like cats or any animals for that matter, she wouldn't even let me have a kitten, and I always wanted one."

Mr. Koble shook his head briefly, and then said, "You would be surprised how often people bequeath money to animal welfare leagues, for the reason that they are..." Mr. Koble's cheeks flushed, and he stopped speaking for a moment. "Of course you may contest the will," he continued, "and you are likely to win. Of course, contesting will take money. Do you have any funds of your own?"

"No, no." Nettie stood up, and then sat down in agitation. "Not a cent. I can't contest the will, it's not the Amish way. I'll be penniless."

Mr. Koble nodded in understanding. "Ah yes, forgive me. The Amish do not contest wills. The Sunnybanks Stray Cat Protection League is still in operation too, after all this time. I checked. But this is prime farming land, surely you can work it?"

It was Nettie's turn to stare at Mr. Koble. "But I have no mules, no plow horses, no balers. I have nothing at all to use for farming the land. It's also neglected and run down, and I'm sure it will need a lot of money spent on it. I'm here all alone, by myself." Nettie took a deep breath to keep the tears at bay. "How can I live? I have no money."

"You could sell the farm, I suppose." Mr. Koble said.

Nettie thought on that for a moment. If she sold the farm, she would have money on which to live, but where would she go? This was the only home she had ever known. *Nee*, she would not be thrown out of her own home. She needed to find work, but what skills did she have? She had a wide knowledge of herbal medicines, but she did not have the trust of anyone in the community. In fact, she didn't even know anyone in the community, not any more. Her *mudder* had made sure of that.

Nettie would need to find work, but how would she get to work? Her horse had been retired; she wasn't even able to drive the buggy anywhere. Sure, there were taxis, but there was no phone in her barn. It was a long walk to the nearest shanty that housed the community phone; she had found that out when she had to walk to call the veterinarian.

Without a buggy horse, she was trapped in the *haus*.

Panic threatened to overwhelm Nettie, and she fought against it.

Nettie decided at that moment that she would keep the farm, no matter what. It was her birthright, and she would not give it up. *Have some backbone*, she said to herself, and then winced as she realized that it had been one of her *mudder's* favorite sayings.

"Miss Swarey, are you all right?"

Nettie came back to the present with a jolt. She wondered how long Mr. Koble had been speaking to her.

"This is all quite a shock."

Mr. Koble simply smiled sympathetically, then stood up and handed her his card. "I'll be in touch. My office has made application for a Letters Testamentary to be issued, as you are the executor of your mother's will."

"Do I need to sign anything now?"

The lawyer shook his head slightly. "No. The will is currently in probate."

Nettie remembered that Mr. Koble had mentioned that word before. "Probate, what's that?"

"Probate is the process by which a will is proved to be valid or invalid in keeping with the laws of the Commonwealth of Pennsylvania." Mr. Koble spoke slowly and said each word clearly.

"Oh, I see." Nettie's head was spinning.

"The Register of Wills will issue you with a Short Certificate."

Nettie simply nodded, not wanting to ask what a Short Certificate was. It made no difference. One thing was clear: she was to inherit the farm and *haus,* and stray cats were to inherit her *mudder's* money.

At any rate, Mr. Koble must have felt it necessary to explain. "A Short Certificate is a document that provides certified proof of the appointment of you as executor of the will, that is, of you as the Estate's Personal Representative. You need it to gain access to the assets, that is, the house and the farm, and so on."

A sudden feeling of apprehension washed over Nettie. "Do you foresee any problems?"

Mr. Koble's bushy eyebrows rose. "No, not at all. It is all very straightforward."

Mr. Koble made a move to the door, and Nettie followed him out, after she set down his card on the table. It was a clear, spring day, but that did not help Nettie's mood, which had turned to despair and was on a rapid downward spiral.

After Mr. Koble drove away in his expensive looking car, Nettie walked onto the road and stood in the sunlight. Sunlight often lifted her mood, but today, so far, it was not helping. She had just turned back to the *haus,* when she heard the clip clop of hooves. *I wonder who could be visiting now?* Nettie thought.

Nettie turned around to see a beautiful, palomino horse trotting toward her. He did not seem frightened, but was simply trotting along. When he reached Nettie, he stopped and nuzzled her hand.

Nettie laughed. "Where have you escaped from, boy?" She stroked his golden neck and his long white mane.

Harry, Nettie's retired buggy horse, called out to the palomino and he answered, whinnying softly. "I'll put you in with Harry and then I'll have to walk all the way to the phone shanty," Nettie told the horse. "Although, who would I call? If I call the bishop, he will visit and ask me a lot more questions. Perhaps I should walk to the Glicks on the neighboring farm and tell them I've found you. Someone must be looking for you." Nettie did not want to visit the Glicks—after her secluded life, she was a little afraid of people, but she could see no other option. At least the Glicks would not ask her as many questions as the bishop had after her *mudder* had died. Sure, the bishop was well intentioned and kindly, but Nettie was not used to people.

Now another problem presented itself; how would she lead the horse to the field? She did not want to leave the horse standing on the road while she went to fetch a headstall, in case he ran away. Nettie suddenly had an idea. She unpinned her prayer *kapp* and wrapped it around the horse's neck. He didn't seem to mind, and followed her willingly to the field, where Harry was delighted to see him.

Then, as the horse trotted away happily, Nettie noticed sweat marks on the horse where a harness had been. "He's a buggy horse!" Nettie said aloud. The horse looked in very good condition, but Nettie did not approve of the sweat marks on the horse. She thought it common sense, let alone good horse keeping skills, that the horse must be brushed thoroughly or washed after being driven in the buggy, to remove all dried sweat marks. What sort of owner did this horse have?

Chapter Four

Nettie was glad of one thing: the horse was a buggy horse, so that would save her a long walk to the shanty to call the bishop, or a long walk to the nearby farm to speak to the Glicks. She would simply drive the horse to the Glicks' *haus*.

Nettie caught the horse, ignoring the complaints of Harry who did not want his new friend to leave, and took him to the barn. She tied him up, and gave him a thorough brushing. Nettie was a little worried that the horse might misbehave in the buggy, so after brushing him, she put the harness on rather carefully. He seemed fine about the harness, so she carefully hitched him to her buggy.

The horse was well behaved throughout, so Nettie led him outside, and walked him around in big circles. Again, he was well-mannered, so Nettie got in the buggy. She asked the horse to walk off slowly, and he did. She walked him around in circles, and made him stop a few times. He stopped very well and Nettie soon felt confident that he was a well trained buggy horse after all, so she set off at a walk in the direction of the Glicks' farm.

Nettie secretly hoped the owner would not be found too soon, as this horse was an answer to prayer. Without a buggy horse, she was trapped at the farm. Perhaps the bishop could arrange for her to borrow a horse from someone, just until she could find work and buy a buggy horse of her own.

Nettie was so lost in thought that, for a while, she did not notice another buggy approaching. She looked up to see a young *mann* driving a buggy pulled by a high stepping, bay horse that snorted and tossed his head when the *mann* pulled him to a stop next to Nettie.

Nettie was taken aback at the black look on the *mann's* face. "What are you doing with my horse?" he yelled.

Nettie was too taken aback to speak, so just sat there with her mouth open, trying to bite back the tears. When the *mann* continued to glare at her, she found her voice. "He just turned up at my *haus*."

"Why are you driving him then? Just because you found him, doesn't mean you can keep him!"

Nettie winced at the accusatory tone in the *mann's* voice. She was fed up with being bullied and yelled at. She'd had years of it with her *mudder*, and now this stranger was accusing her of being a horse thief, when all she was trying to do was to do the right thing, to find the horse's owner.

A wave of indignation swept over her. "Now see here," she said in a commanding tone. "How dare you accuse me of wrongdoing! This horse turned up outside my *haus*, and as my only buggy horse is lame and has had to be retired, I had no way of contacting anyone to tell them I'd found him. I couldn't drive my own horse, so I harnessed up this horse and I was on my way to the Glicks to tell them that I'd found him."

The *mann* looked taken aback at Nettie's manner. "Why didn't you call someone? Don't you have a phone in your barn?" His tone was less accusatory and more enquiring.

"*Nee*, I do not," Nettie snapped. "And it's a long walk to the phone shanty, as I found out when my buggy horse went lame and I had to call the veterinarian to him. Besides, you should be thanking me for finding your horse." Nettie was fuming at the *mann's* manner; how dare he speak to her like that!

As the *mann* opened his mouth to speak, Nettie remembered the harness marks on the horse. "Besides, I also brushed your horse. You should be ashamed of yourself leaving a horse with sweat marks."

The *mann* gasped, and his face went from a fading red to a deep shade of purple. "For your information, I tied him up and was about to wash him, but when I came back outside the barn, I found him missing. I then harnessed up this horse and went in search of him."

"Oh." Nettie was glad to hear he had intended to wash the horse, but his manner with people left a lot to be desired. "Well," she said, "you can follow me back to my *haus* and then take your horse." Her voice shook when she said that, with the realization that she had no buggy horse after all.

"Where is your *haus*?" The *mann* looked less angry now.

Nettie waved her hand in the general direction of her farm. "I'm Nettie Swarey."

The *mann* once again looked shocked. "Oh. Well, I'm sorry to hear about your *mudder*."

"*Denki*."

The *mann* took a moment to settle his horse which was pawing the ground and snorting. "I'm Daniel Glick."

Nettie simply nodded.

"And your horse is lame?" he asked.

"*Jah*, and the veterinarian said he must be retired."

"And he's your only horse?"

"*Jah*," Nettie said again, wondering where Daniel Glick was going with this line of questioning.

"Why don't you borrow the horse then? You're most welcome to. I have this horse as you see, and I don't need two horses."

Nettie's response was automatic. "*Denki*, but *nee*, I couldn't possibly do that." She silently rebuked herself for saying that; this would be an answer to prayer.

"It would make me feel better for the rude way I spoke to you, and you'd be doing me a favor," Daniel continued. "He's a very good buggy horse, but he likes to be in work and I don't have time to drive him. My own horse here is highly strung and needs a lot of work to keep him calm." As if on cue, Daniel's horse arched his neck and pawed the ground angrily. "You'd be doing me a favor, actually," he repeated.

Nettie thought for a moment. She had prayed to *Gott* to find her another buggy horse, and it seemed as if He had. She should accept the provision of *Gott* gracefully. "*Denki*, that is very kind of you," she said meekly. "It might be some time before I can get another buggy horse, though."

Daniel waved her concerns away. "Keep him as long as you like," he said. "By the way, his name is Blessing."

Daniel watched the girl drive away at a trot, admiring the fact that she had harnessed up a strange buggy horse and driven him. Why, for all the girl knew, the horse could have had any manner of behavioral problems and even been dangerous. She had courage to harness a strange horse and drive him on the road.

Yet Daniel was surprised at Nettie Swarey herself. He had imagined her much older, and far less attractive, what with some of the local *Englischer* schoolchildren referring to her as 'an old witch.' When he had gotten over the initial shock of seeing someone driving his lost horse, he had been surprised to see that the driver was a pretty, round-faced, blonde girl, with a creamy complexion and deep, blue eyes. *Wary eyes*, he said to himself, and then chuckled when he remembered how she had stood up to him.

He was embarrassed over his implication that she had stolen the horse, but the shy, retiring, secretive Nettie Swarey he had heard about was not the same girl who had dressed him down for falsely accusing her and for leaving harness marks on his horse.

Daniel laughed aloud, and then smiled to himself all the way back to the Glicks' farm.

Chapter Five

Nettie had spent a pleasant week. She had scrubbed the *haus* from top to bottom and had added lavender to the washing water, so the *haus* was well on its way to losing its musty smell. She was happy that she now had means of transport. She would just have to have faith that *Gott* would help her to find work. For now, she had a supply of food in the *haus*, there was plenty of grazing for her two horses, and there was ample grain stored in the barn. Her financial situation would have to be addressed, but it was not urgent.

Nettie was out in the garden, gathering the tiny, purple-dotted, white flowers as well as the stems of chickweed to make a salve. Her *mudder* had found that it provided relief for her arthritis, but Nettie liked to have the salve on hand for insect stings as well as burns.

The clip clop of horse's shoes signaled a visitor, and Nettie looked up, hoping it would be Daniel Glick. She had found him strangely attractive, despite his rude ways, and he had made her heart flutter. Yet this was no handsome bay, high-stepping horse approaching, but a rather tired looking, shaggy, gray horse, and even at the distance, Nettie could see that the *mann* had dark hair, unlike the fair hair of Daniel Glick.

Nettie wiped her hands on her apron and stepped outside the herb garden to meet the *mann*. The *mann* drove straight up to her, and got out of the buggy, taking the horse by the bridle. He nodded to Nettie. "*Gude mariye*."

Nettie said a polite *good morning* back, and wondered what the *mann* wanted.

The *mann* smiled at her, a thin, tight-lipped smile. "Nettie, don't you recognize me?"

Nettie gasped and clutched at her throat. "Jebediah Sprinkler!" she exclaimed. *How long has it been?* she wondered. *Five, six years?*

"What are you doing here? Why have you come back?" Nettie had a horrible feeling of apprehension which formed a hard knot in the pit of her stomach.

"I'm sorry to hear about your *mudder*," Jebediah said.

"*Denki*." Nettie studied him. His face had hard lines. He would not have been much older than she, yet he looked many years older.

"Nettie, can we talk?"

"*Jah*, go on."

Jebediah looked annoyed. "*Nee*, I mean in the *haus*."

Nettie suddenly felt afraid. "*Nee*, Jebediah, I'm here alone and that wouldn't be right."

Jebediah appeared to consider her words for a moment. "If you wish. Nettie, there's no way to break the news to you gently, but I have to tell you that your *mudder* left the *haus* and *farm* to me."

Nettie stared blankly at him. Firstly, there was the shock of Jebediah Sprinkler turning up without warning after all these years, and now he was saying he owned her property. "But, but," she stammered, "the lawyer said it was all left to me."

Jebediah did not appear concerned by her words. "You're speaking of an old will, of course."

Nettie scratched her head. "What do you mean?"

"The will," Jebediah said, with a hint of annoyance in his voice. "The lawyer had an old will."

"Well, *jah*, he did." Nettie wondered how Jebediah knew.

Jebediah looked smug and smirked a little. "Your *mudder* made a new one after that."

"Why didn't the lawyer know about it, then?"

Jebediah shrugged. "How should I know? Look, Nettie, your *mudder* made a new will leaving everything to me. I'm surprised she didn't tell you. Are you sure she didn't mention the will to you? She didn't say anything at all about it?"

"*Nee*, she didn't tell me, and why would she leave anything to you?" Nettie felt she was becoming hysterical, but it was all too much to process. What was Jebediah up to?

"We were engaged at the time," Jebediah said

sternly, "and your *mudder* obviously thought we would be married."

Nettie shuddered at the memory. Her *mudder* had all but arranged a marriage between Jebediah and Nettie, when Nettie was sixteen. Jebediah's *mudder* was an old friend of Nettie's *mudder*, and the two of them had decided that their *kinner* should be married. Jebediah had also been keen for them to marry, but Nettie had refused outright. It was the only time she had disobeyed her *mudder*, and her *mudder* had been furious with her. Nettie had thought her *mudder* had made her life a misery before that time, but it was nothing to the way she was treated afterwards.

Nettie had always found Jebediah to be a cold person, perhaps even cruel, and there was no way she would subject herself to marrying him. She had somehow managed to find the backbone at the time to stand up to her *mudder*.

Nettie thought it would not have been out of character for her *mudder* to leave the *haus* and farm to Jebediah in the will. In fact, her *mudder* had often brought up Jebediah's name, saying he was not yet married and Nettie should reconsider. That was, at least, until Jebediah's *mudder* passed away and Nettie's *mudder* of course stopped receiving letters from her.

Perhaps her *mudder* had in fact left a will leaving everything to Jebediah. It would have been her way of trying to force Nettie to marry him after all. Yet why wouldn't her *mudder* mention that to Nettie, and why did she not sign the will with her lawyer? That part made no sense.

Nettie looked up to see Jebediah looking at her through narrowed eyes. "My *mudder* never mentioned any such will to me," she said.

"That doesn't change the fact that she made one."

"Do you have a copy?" Nettie held her breath.

"*Nee*. I assume it's somewhere in the *haus*."

"Why didn't she lodge it with her lawyer, the one who she made the, *err*, other will with?" Nettie winced as she said 'other' will.

"I'm not your *mudder's* keeper," Jebediah said in a hostile voice. "How should I know? All I know is that she told me she had made a will in favor of me, leaving me the *haus* and the farm. Perhaps she lodged it with another lawyer."

Nettie was growing more and more anxious. "Even if she did, Jebediah, that was because she thought we were getting married. We didn't get married."

Jebediah took a step toward Nettie and she took a step back. "Listen to me," he said, his voice hard. "Your *mudder* made a will naming me as the sole beneficiary. That's a fact, and nothing you say can change that. I want my inheritance, so I'm going to start to call all the lawyers in the district. There is no need for you to search the *haus* for the will, but do let me know if you happen to find it. I'm staying with the Glock *familye*; you can reach me there if you wish to speak to me."

Nettie stomped her foot. "I will destroy it," she said in a raised voice.

Jebediah narrowed his eyes, and his face and neck turned went a horrid shade of beet red. "*Nee*, you will not," he said, in an obvious temper. He moved toward Nettie and she was afraid what he would do, but just then, the buggy horse Blessing trotted over to them, startling Jebediah.

Jebediah flung up his arm as the horse made to nip him. He jumped back aboard his buggy and took up the reins, while muttering about dangerous horses. "Nettie, you know you have to do the right thing by *Gott*," he said patiently, as if speaking to a child. "Your *mudder* left the inheritance to me, and you must abide by her wishes. Otherwise, you are working against the will of *Gott*." With that, he hit his horse hard with the reins and the horse trotted off.

Nettie stood there, watching after him. She was quite shaken up. Thank goodness Blessing had come along when he did, as that had made Jebediah leave. Nettie now turned her attention to Blessing. "How did you get out?" she asked him, and then looked over to see the gate was open. Nettie would never leave the gate to a field open, so she wondered if Blessing was one of those horses that could open gates. She took hold of a piece of Blessing's long mane, and he followed her meekly back to the field. Nettie shut the gate, and then went into the barn looking for something to secure the gate in case the horse was indeed able to lift the latch.

Jebediah was right about it being the will of Gott, she thought with sadness in her heart, *if*

Mamm really did make a will leaving the haus and farm to him. It would be the will of Gott to honor the terms of any will.

Still, Nettie had rebellious thoughts. It was not fair. She had looked after her invalid *mudder* for all these years, only to have the possibility of eviction hanging over her. If she did find a will, what would she do? She was tempted to destroy it. Such thoughts surprised Nettie, for she had always strived to do the right thing.

Chapter Six

Nettie was tired and in despair. She had spent a restless night tossing and turning, struggling with her conscience, wondering what she would do if there was a will in favor of Jebediah Sprinkler.

If she found the will, what would she do? She wanted to destroy it, but that was not the honorable thing to do. Still, if she did the honorable thing, she would have nowhere to live. The bishop would find her a *familye* to live with, no doubt, but what sort of life would that be for her?

Nettie had come to no conclusion, and had begun her search of the *haus*. The *haus* itself might not have been large by Amish *familye* standards, but it was large nonetheless. It was a renovated 1700s farmhouse, and unusually for an Amish *haus*, was packed full of items such as crocheted doilies, crocheted rugs, and all manner of knitted items. Most of these were tucked away in aged, yellowing boxes of every size and shape. Old, plain chests of drawers were crammed full of old knitted or crocheted items, and the kitchen cupboards were full of kitchen utensils. Nettie guessed that most were her *grossmammi's*, or even her *grossmammi's* before her. Her own *mudder* had been somewhat of a hoarder; she had thrown nothing out, even if it had been broken. Her *mudder* thought that women should be knitting or crocheting all day long when not doing chores, always quoting a favorite Amish saying, "Idleness is a resting-pillow of the devil and a cause of all sorts of wickedness."

Nettie figured she could have many weeks' work ahead of her. If there was in fact a will leaving the farm to Jebediah Sprinkler, it could be tucked away in one of the boxes. Nettie had no idea what she would do if and when she found the will, but her first job was to find the will.

Nettie sat down to a breakfast of stewed crackers in warm milk, followed by sausage and scrapple topped with apple butter. Nettie had liked scrapple since she was a child, and it was the only meat her mother could eat, being soft. Scrapple was pork scraps and trimmings combined with flour, cornmeal, and sage from the herb garden, and then formed into a loaf. Nettie always cut it into three-quarter-inch slices and pan-fried it until it was brown to form a crust, but she had not fried it for her *mudder*.

She'd only had a mug of *kaffi* before she'd milked the goat, fed the chickens, and started her search of the *haus*. Now, with some food in her stomach, Nettie was able to think more clearly. She would call the lawyer and inform him of Jebediah Sprinkler's attempted claim on the will. The lawyer would be able to advise her.

Nettie decided to harness up Blessing and drive him to the phone shanty. She took the lawyer's card from the table on her way out. The card was fancy, with gold embossed letters on a white background with plenty of swirls. Nettie wondered why anyone would spend so much money on something that could have been just as effective if simple.

It was a beautiful, late spring day, and Nettie's spirits lifted as she drove Blessing in the direction of the phone shanty. She was about to turn down the lane, but spotted a buggy at the end of it, right near the phone shanty. Someone else was making a call. Nettie drew

Blessing to a stop and pondered her options. If she continued ahead, to the phone shanty, she would have to make small talk to the people there, and Nettie, having been used to isolation, dreaded social encounters. On the other hand, should she drive Blessing to the Glicks' *haus*? Nettie knew they had a phone in their barn, as her *mudder* often complained about that fact. Yet did she want to speak to the Glicks any more than whoever was currently at the phone shanty?

The thought of running into Daniel Glick sent butterflies racing through Nettie's stomach, but as she hesitated, trying to decide, Blessing took the option out of her hands. Without any encouragement, Blessing set off at a trot in the direction of the Glicks' *haus*. *He's probably heading for home*, Nettie thought with resignation, letting Blessing trot on ahead.

Nettie enjoyed the drive to the Glick *haus*, out in the spring air, the buggy winding its way down little used roads amidst a backdrop of gently rolling hills, past beautiful, golden, corn fields and green alfalfa crops.

As Nettie approached the Glick *haus*, she saw Daniel standing next to a pretty, young woman with dark hair showing in front of her prayer *kapp*. Nettie was unprepared for the pangs of jealousy that assaulted her. *What's wrong with me?* she silently scolded herself. *I hope I'm not turning into one of those desperate women that Mamm was always complaining about.*

Nettie drew Blessing to a halt and Daniel walked over to the buggy, followed by the attractive, young woman.

"*Hiya*, Daniel." Nettie smiled shyly at Daniel and then at the young woman.

"*Hullo*, Nettie. Do you member my *schweschder*, Melissa?"

"*Schweschder?*"

"Yes, who else would she be?" Daniel's green

eyes were twinkling with amusement and Nettie hoped that her relief had not shown in her voice. Anyway, whatever was she thinking to be so attracted to this young *mann*?

"*Jah*, I remember you, Melissa, but you look different."

Melissa laughed heartedly. "Well, it's been many years since we were small *kinner*. You look different too."

Nettie at once warmed to Melissa. "I need to call my lawyer, so may I use your phone, please? I drove to the shanty but someone was already there."

"*Jah*, of course," both Daniel and Melissa said together.

Nettie climbed down from the buggy and Daniel tied up Blessing for her. "How is Blessing going for you?" His eyes were kind, and her stomach fluttered at his close proximity.

"*Wunderbaar*, *denki*," Nettie said, twisting the strands of her prayer *kapp*.

"Please feel free to come and use our phone at any time," Daniel said. "I'll show you where it is."

Nettie followed Daniel and Melissa over to the barn. Every time Nettie looked at Melissa, she was smiling warmly at her, so Nettie forgot her nervousness about being in a social situation. "I'm sorry about your *mudder*," Melissa said.

"*Denki*."

"Are you lonely?"

Nettie looked at Melissa with surprise. "Lonely?"

"*Jah*. The bishop told everyone not to visit you until you were ready; he said you'd be too overwhelmed."

Nettie saw Daniel shoot Melissa a warning

look, so hurried to reassure him. She did not want Melissa to get into trouble on her account. "That was kind of the bishop. My *mudder* did not permit visitors and she did not permit me to leave the *haus*, so it's left me a little, well, shy."

"May I visit you some time?"

This time Daniel verbally rebuked his *schweschder*. "Melissa!"

Melissa hung her head. "Sorry, Nettie."

"I would love you to visit, Melissa, *denki*." Nettie meant it. She had felt an instant kinship with Melissa and was sure the two of them would get along well. It would be lovely to have a *gut* friend, one close to her own age, when the only companionship she'd had for years was her *mudder*.

Melissa left the barn, smiling, and Daniel turned to Nettie. "Please forgive my *schweschder*. She's very forthright and always speaks her mind. Don't feel pressured into having her visit."

Nettie smiled. "I really like Melissa. I look forward to her visits."

Daniel looked at Nettie as if trying to ascertain whether she was simply being polite or whether she actually meant it. He didn't comment, but showed her to the phone. "Here you are. Please feel free to come and use it anytime. Now I'll give you some privacy."

When Daniel left, Nettie stared at the phone. A dreadful feeling of anxiety settled over her.

Chapter Seven

Nettie was relieved that her lawyer, Mr. Koble, was in the office, and was able to speak to her after just a short time on hold. After relaying that everything Jebediah Sprinkler had said to her, she waited nervously to hear what Mr. Koble had to say.

"Sprinkler, is that an Amish name? I've never heard it before."

Nettie frowned. That was the last thing she thought that the lawyer would say. "I have no idea, but I think his father came over from

Germany. I'm not too sure. I only know that his mother was Amish." Nettie wondered what that had to do with anything, but thought it impolite to ask him.

"Why would your mother think to leave anything to this man?"

Nettie looked around nervously, but there was no one in sight, apart from two chickens scratching around outside the barn door. "We were engaged when I was sixteen," she said in a low voice. "My mother tried to force me to marry him."

There was silence on the other end of the phone, and Nettie said, "Mr. Koble?"

"Yes, I see," he said. "Obviously, there is no record of any such will here and I know nothing of it."

Nettie's spirits lifted for a moment. "Does that mean the will isn't registered?"

Mr. Koble's words soon dashed her hopes.

"No. Wills are only registered *after* the testator is deceased, not before. I registered this will at the Register of Wills at the Courthouse in Duke Street."

"What if the will leaving everything to Jebediah Sprinkler is found?" Nettie held her breath, waiting for the answer.

"Do you mean will it take precedence over the will I have just registered?" Without waiting for Nettie to answer, Mr. Koble continued. "Yes, it will, only if it was written *after* this will. And as this will was written before you were sixteen, if the will that allegedly leaves everything to Sprinkler is found, then yes, he will be the beneficiary."

Nettie clutched at her throat, and tears filled her eyes.

"You could, of course, contest the will," Mr. Koble advised, "but I know that the Amish do not contest wills, and you have already decided not to contest the funds going to the stray cat rescue league."

"That's right," Nettie said in a small voice.

"And clearly this Mr. Sprinkler has not been able to produce the will?"

"No, he says my mother must have it in the house somewhere. Mr. Koble, do you think there is such a will?"

"There is no evidence either way at this stage," Mr. Koble said in his sensible, lawyer voice. "Yet the will in my possession was not revoked. It is usual to revoke a will if a later will has been made. That suggests to me that this man's claim might be fraudulent. At any rate, let me know at once if you do happen to find a will. Goodbye, Miss Swarey."

"Oh, just one more thing."

"Yes?"

"What would happen if, err, if the will

somehow got destroyed?" Nettie was shocked that she had even asked. Verbalizing what she had been considering somehow made it seem far more real.

"It is a felony criminal offense to destroy or hide a will." The lawyer's voice was stern.

"Oh yes, thank you, Mr. Koble." Nettie hung up and walked out into the sun. Daniel was over by the *haus* and when Nettie walked out, he walked toward her.

"Is everything okay, I hope?" He looked somewhat embarrassed, and then added, "I'm sorry; I don't mean to pry."

Nettie smiled. "*Nee*, that's fine. A *mann* by the name of Jebediah Sprinkler—he was an old friend of my *mudder's*—came to visit me the other day, and said that he was the sole beneficiary of her will." Daniel gasped, but Nettie kept talking. "He doesn't have a copy of the will, but said my *mudder* must have put it somewhere in the *haus*."

Daniel was visibly shocked. "Could that be true?"

Nettie shrugged. "My lawyer doesn't think so, as the current will wasn't revoked, but it's a possibility."

"And the current will left everything to you, I assume?"

Nettie tried not to cry. "*Nee*, only the *haus* and the farm. My *mudder* left all the money to a stray cat protection league."

Daniel gasped yet again. "But why would your *mudder* leave this *mann* the farm and the money?"

Nettie hesitated. She did not want to go into the whole story of her *mudder* trying to pressure her to marry Jebediah Sprinkler; in fact, Daniel was the last person she wanted to tell. Thankfully, Melissa chose this moment to hurry out of the *haus*.

"Nettie," she said breathlessly, after running

over to her, "*Mamm* wants to invite you to come to dinner next week."

"*Denki*," Nettie said, nervous at the prospect of being around several people at once, and at the same time, nervous at the prospect of being in the same room as Daniel.

Melissa smiled, looked at Daniel and then at Nettie, and then hurried back into the *haus*.

Alone with Daniel once again, Nettie was afraid that his questioning would pick up where it had left off, but he seemed to have other things on his mind.

"You will have no income?"

Nettie shook her head. "*Nee*, that's why I'm looking for work. *Denki* for letting me use your phone and *denki* for letting me borrow Blessing too. He's been, well, a blessing."

They both laughed, and Nettie relaxed somewhat. "So you haven't found work yet?" Daniel asked, his voice full of concern.

"Not yet, but I'm sure I will."

Daniel rubbed his chin. "Your *mudder* left you the farm as well as the *haus*?"

"*Jah*, she left everything to me, the *haus*, the farm, the furniture, absolutely everything, with the exception of her money."

"Have you thought about working the farm?"

"But, but," Nettie spluttered, "How could I? There's only me, and there are no plows, balers, mules, plow horses, anything!"

Daniel chuckled. "Sorry, that came out wrong. Your farm adjoins ours. We have fifteen acres of corn, fifteen acres of wheat, and twenty acres of alfalfa. The demand for alfalfa is increasing so much that we can't keep up with it. My *vadder* has been looking to lease more land for alfalfa, but hasn't found anywhere suitable yet. This is just an idea that's only just occurred to me, but would you consider leasing your farm to us?"

“But the whole farm’s run down and the fencing is in poor repair.”

“I don’t think the alfalfa will try to escape.” Daniel chuckled again. “If you agree, I’ll tell *Datt* and see what he has to say, as he has to approve it, of course. Anyway, we’re familiar with your land as it’s right next to ours, and that would cut our costs considerably.”

Nettie beamed. This could be the answer to her financial troubles. She could scarcely believe it. Then again, Nettie figured, she had prayed to *Gott* to provide for her; what was the point of praying if one did not expect *Gott* to answer? Nettie sent up a silent prayer of thanks to *Gott* for his provision. Yet, as soon as she did, Nettie immediately worried that the will that was leaving everything to Jebediah Sprinkler would come to light. *I have to have more faith*, she thought. *I must rely on Gott*.

~

Daniel watched Nettie disappear from view. He hoped she would consider leasing the farm to his *familye*, and he was sure his *vadder* would be overjoyed at the chance to lease the adjoining farming land. It was good soil, and had lain fallow for many years.

Yet Daniel had an ulterior motive. He was attracted to Nettie. She appeared to be everything he wanted in a woman. *Steady on*, he said to himself, *you don't know her well enough yet, not by a long way*.

Nevertheless, leasing the land would help his *familye*, and it would help Nettie. She wouldn't have to go out and find work. Daniel felt anxious at the thought of Nettie out amongst *Englischers*. Everyone in the community knew about the girl whose *mudder* had refused to allow visitors to come to the *haus* for years, and who had kept her *dochder* in virtual seclusion. Daniel was surprised that Nettie was as outgoing as she was. She must be of strong character to have withstood all that and come out unscathed.

Daniel's thoughts turned to the will, and the stranger who had arrived at Nettie's, claiming that he was the sole beneficiary of her *mudder's* will. Something was not right there, of that Daniel was sure. This *mann* was clearly someone who was trying to take advantage of Nettie. "Not if I can help it," Daniel said aloud. He felt protective toward Nettie—and something more.

Chapter Eight

Nettie could not remember ever having gone out to someone's place for dinner. Surely she and her *mudder* would have gone to dinner at someone's *haus* when she was younger, but try as she might, she could not remember such an occasion.

Nettie had washed and ironed her green dress to wear to the Glicks' *haus*. She also starched her prayer *kapp* and apron. She was determined to make a *gut* impression on the Glicks. Nettie wondered what the Glicks might know about her. Much to her embarrassment, everyone at the funeral seemed to have some knowledge of her *mudder's* strange ways.

As she dressed for dinner, Nettie recalled how her heart had skipped a beat when she had seen Daniel speaking to an attractive girl. She was pleased that the girl happened to be his *schweschder.* She wondered if Daniel did have a girl that he was fond of. Maybe she would find out at dinner tonight. Surely he would have a girl already, a handsome *mann* like that.

Having no mirror in the *haus,* she went to the kitchen, took out a shiny, large, frying pan, and held it in front of her face to study her reflection. Nettie considered her best feature to be her blue eyes. They were a clear blue, not a gray blue or a hazel blue, but a clear blue like the sky.

She ran her hand over the roundness of her face, pleased that she had long since grown out of the spots that had troubled her as a teenager. She pushed stray hairs of blonde hair back under her *kapp.* Her *mudder* had caught her looking at herself in the frying pan once and she was scolded for it; her *mudder* had screamed at her and called her prideful.

"That's the best I can do," she said to herself. She often spoke aloud to herself, and had even done so when her *mudder* was alive. Her *mudder* was not someone she could speak to as one would speak to a friend, so she would speak to herself when she was in the *haus,* and when she was outside, she would tell her troubles to her horse.

Pangs of nerves rippled through Nettie's stomach. What would she speak about at dinner? Earlier in the day she had baked a rhubarb pie to take to the Glicks', but now she was worrying if that was the done thing. Should she take something with her if someone invited her to dinner? It felt right to do so. Nettie hushed the questions that were flying through her head about dinner protocol. *Goodness me, Nettie, it's just dinner*, she scolded herself, trying to push away her nerves.

Nettie harnessed up Blessing and made her way to the Glicks. She was careful to lock every door and every window in the *haus* before she left, just in case Jebediah Sprinkler might get the idea in his head to snoop around. She remembered that her *mudder* had told her with disapproval that most Amish did not have locks. There had been no sign of Jebediah, but Nettie wasn't taking any chances. As she drove along, Nettie realized what Daniel meant about Blessing loving being worked. He trotted along happily as though he were thoroughly enjoying herself. Blessing would not be happy just to be in a field; that was clear enough. He loved attention, and he loved trotting down the narrow ribbons of roads that made their way between the farms. As they neared the Glicks' *haus*, Blessing trotted a little faster. *He must have happy memories of this place,* Nettie thought. *Clearly, Daniel is kind to his animals.*

Daniel appeared in front of her as she pulled up near the Glicks' barn.

"Blessing looks happy."

"*Jah*, he enjoys the work; I can tell that."

"How are you today, Nettie?"

"I'm well, Daniel. And you?"

Daniel nodded. "Fine, *denki*."

As Nettie got out of the buggy, she said, "*Ach*, I almost forgot. I made a pie."

"I love pie."

Nettie laughed and then stopped herself when she realized that it had been many years since she had heard the sound of her own laughter. "It's a rhubarb pie."

"*Wunderbaar*." Daniel smiled at her, and led her to the *haus*.

Nettie smiled; it was nice to think of something other than her *mudder* and what might cause her to have one of her tantrums.

Mrs. Glick was at the door by the time they reached the front porch. "Hello, Nettie. Nice to see you again. I'm sorry I didn't get to speak to you at the funeral."

"Hello, Mrs. Glick. I'm afraid I didn't really speak to anyone much at the funeral." Nettie quickly changed the subject. "It was nice of you to invite me to dinner." Nettie handed her the pie.

"You didn't have to bring anything."

"It's a rhubarb pie."

"That's Mr. Glick's favorite." Mrs. Glick turned to Daniel. "Sit down with Nettie until dinner's ready."

"Let me help you with something." Nettie was not used to being waited on, and she was a little nervous about being alone with Daniel.

"*Nee*, have a seat and relax."

Daniel motioned for her to walk through the next doorway. She walked through to a huge room. Daniel's *daed* was sitting on a large sofa near a corner. After they greeted each other, Nettie sat down.

Mr. Glick had a newspaper in his hands. He placed it down on the table next to him. "I hear you're looking after Blessing."

Nettie shot a look at Daniel who gave her a quick smile. "*Jah*, he's a fine horse and he came along at just the right time. My other horse had just gone lame and now he can't work anymore."

Even though he was seated, Nettie could see that Mr. Glick was a large man. His hair was balding, but she could see some of the features of Daniel in his face. They had the same straight nose, the chiseled mouth, and the well shaped ears. *Maybe Mr. Glick was also good-looking in his day,* Nettie thought.

"Daniel says you're looking for work?"

"That's right." Nettie took it as a *gut* sign that Daniel had obviously spoken of her to his parents.

"What kind of work?"

Nettie looked down at her hands as if looking at them would somehow stop them fidgeting. "I'm not trained to do anything at all. I don't really know what I could do. I like to cook and I can sew."

"Would you mind if I enquire on your behalf with people I know?"

"*Denki*, I would appreciate it very much if you could." Nettie at once felt at home with all the Glicks. She had immediately warmed to Daniel's *schweschder,* and his *daed* was just as welcoming as his *mudder.* She looked around the room; it was neat and well ordered. Colorful, crocheted rugs covered the backs of the three sofas.

"*Hiya*, Nettie." Daniel's *schweschder,* Melissa, greeted Nettie as she came into the room. She settled into the sofa next to her *daed.* "*Mamm* sent me out of the kitchen to tell everyone that dinner will be ready in five minutes."

"It smells delicious," Nettie said.

"It's roasted chicken and a beef stew."

"That'll do me," Daniel said with a smile.

Nettie was glad that dinner would be only five minutes away. She had no idea what to say. Her worst fear was that she would sit in silence through the entire dinner and the Glicks would think her a little odd. She had to think of something to say, but what do people speak about at times like these?

Thankfully, Daniel spoke first. “It was a beautiful day today, wasn’t it?”

“*Jah*, I love this time of year. I don’t like it when it’s really cold. I much prefer the sunshine.”

“*Nee*, I like the cold because we can go ice-skating. Do you like ice-skating, Nettie?”

How could she tell him, without looking foolish, that her *mudder* had never allowed her to ice-skate? She would have to say it boldly and not in a timid voice. She turned to Daniel and looked him in the eyes. “I have never ice-skated.”

“Never?”

She shook her head.

“You must come with us then, Nettie,” Melissa said. “I can teach you.”

“Will you come with us in winter?” Daniel asked.

Nettie smiled and nodded. She had always wanted to join in the games, the volleyball, the ice-skating and even the singings, but she was never allowed to do anything that would be enjoyable. Her *mudder* had always found some reason why she could not join in with others. The only thing her *mudder* had ever been keen for her to do was marry someone whom Nettie found entirely unsuitable.

Chapter Nine

"Dinner must be ready by now," Mr. Glick said as he rose from the sofa.

"*Jah*, come on, Nettie. You can sit next to me," Melissa said.

Nettie followed Melissa to the dinner table.

After they said their silent prayers, they filled their plates with the food from the center of the table.

Nettie considered she had covered her nervousness well while speaking to the Glicks in the living room and she hoped that she would be able to do the same throughout dinner. Nettie was pleased that she had an invitation to go skating with them, even though it was months away. Skating had always seemed so much fun.

Mrs. Glick's voice broke through her thoughts. "Nettie, you've hardly put anything on your plate. Here, have some more chicken. You have to keep up your strength." Mrs. Glick passed the plate full of chicken pieces to Nettie.

Nettie took another piece. "*Denki*. I do like the way you cooked the chicken, Mrs. Glick."

"It's a *familye* recipe," Melissa said.

"A secret recipe?" Nettie asked, with a smile on her face.

Mrs. Glick laughed. "*Nee*, you can have the recipe if you'd like. I'll let you know what's in it after dinner." She looked at her husband. "I don't want to bore the men folk by talking about recipes."

"For once." Daniel laughed.

"It can't be easy for you to live all by yourself, Nettie, with no one to help you with all the chores," Mrs. Glick continued.

Nettie gave a little laugh, which to her dismay came out as more of a choking sound. "I'm used to it. *Mamm* was sick for so long that she wasn't able to do anything." Nettie did not like to say it, but she did find herself with loads of free time now her *mudder* had passed.

"Is it true that your *mudder* wouldn't let people visit?" Melissa asked.

Mrs. Glick clanged her fork on the table. "Melissa, you should not say such things. It's none of your business." Her tone was scolding.

"That's all right, Mrs. Glick. My *mudder* was a strange lady, I guess. She didn't like people coming to the *haus*. I'm not sure why, and if someone knocked on the door, she wouldn't allow me to answer it." Guilt ate away at Nettie, guilt at giving away her *mudder's* secret habits. She looked up at the Glicks. Mr. Glick was looking into his food, and he slowly shook his head. Mrs. Glick was staring at her, as were Daniel and Melissa.

"That's weird," Melissa said looking at her *mudder*. "I'm sorry, *Mamm,* but I do think it's a little weird."

Daniel turned to Nettie. "Forgive my *schweschder*. She's a little outspoken at times and doesn't know when to hold her peace."

"I don't mind," Nettie said. "Everyone knew what my *mudder* was like. She did become quite a recluse at the end and forced me to be the same." Nettie lowered her eyes. She had hoped they would speak of more pleasant things.

"I drove past your *haus* today and noticed how pretty your garden is," Daniel said.

"*Jah*, I love gardening. The irises in the front are just coming out now and the daffodils have been out for some time."

Mr. Glick put down his knife. "Would you take a part-time job gardening, Nettie?"

"That would be perfect for me. Do you know of someone who needs a gardener?"

"We could use someone to help in the garden, couldn't we, Ursula?"

Mrs. Glick beamed. "*Jah*, we certainly could. I don't like the garden. I have allergies and I get rashes from some of the plants. So it's just Melissa to look after our huge garden, but she works three days a week."

"Please say you'll do it, Nettie. It'll be such fun and I can help you on my days off," Melissa said.

"I'd very much like that. *Denki*."

Mr. Glick looked pleased. "*Gut*, you can work out the times with Ursula."

Nettie pondered for a moment if she should offer Mrs. Glick a remedy, and then finally got up the courage to do so. "Mrs. Glick, would you like me to make you a herbal remedy for your allergies? A combination of black cohosh, chickweed, fenugreek, and ginger should bring you relief."

"Why, *denki*, how kind of you, Nettie."

Nettie found it hard to keep the smile from her face. She'd found a new friend in Melissa as well as the rest of the Glick *familye* and *Gott* had provided her with a job. Now all she needed to do was to find and destroy the new will, and then she would be happy.

Mrs. Glick and Melissa cleared the plates, Mrs. Glick again refusing Nettie's offer of help, and then the pair soon returned with chocolate cake over which had been spooned generous dollops of cornstarch pudding and then topped with nutmeg, along with liberal helpings of Nettie's rhubarb pie.

Everyone complimented Nettie on the pie, which made her go bright red, as her *mudder* had always said that vanity was the tool of the devil. Nettie had no idea how to accept a compliment, so simply said "*denki*" in a small voice and then ducked her head.

When they had finished the meal, Mr. Glick spoke up. "Nettie, Daniel mentioned to me the possibility of leasing your land. Would you be interested in that?"

"*Jah*, most certainly," Nettie said, quite pleased.

"I do realize you have to wait until probate is through until we can come to an agreement, but I wanted to make the offer first. I will be sure to pay you well."

"*Denki*," Nettie said, "but I must warn you

that there is a slim possibility that my land might be taken away from me."

Mr. Glick nodded, and looked concerned. "*Jah*, Daniel mentioned that a *mann* had told you that your *mudder* had made a new will leaving everything to him."

Nettie nodded. "My lawyer knows nothing of that will, though, and I suppose if it hasn't been found when probate is through, then it won't matter." *Or if I find the will and destroy it*, Nettie thought.

"Leave it all in the hands of *Gott*," Mr. Glick said, waving his hand in the air nonchalantly.

It's easy for him to say; he isn't in danger of being homeless, Nettie thought unkindly, and then immediately felt guilty. She had in fact been intending to take it out of *Gott's* hands and into her own. If she found the will, what would she do; could she really destroy it?

Chapter Ten

Nettie was on her hands and knees, looking under furniture for the missing will. She swept under the furniture regularly, but now wondered if her *mudder* might have attached a box to the underside of the furniture. She had not uncovered anything by the time she heard a horse trotting up the road.

At first Nettie's heart skipped a beat, wondering if it might be Daniel Glick, then her elation was replaced with anxiety - what if it was Jebediah Sprinkler? And if it was Daniel

Glick, she was covered in dust and did not look her best. Nettie hauled herself off the floor, rubbed her sore knees, and hurried out the front door. The bishop, Mr. Beiler, was just pulling his horse to a stop, and his *fraa*, Linda, was sitting next to him. They both smiled when they saw Nettie.

Nettie did not know whether to be pleased or alarmed. The bishop was likely to tell her that she should attend church meetings, and she didn't know if she was ready for a roomful of people quite yet.

So, with some trepidation, Nettie greeted the bishop and his *fraa* and showed them both inside. "Would you like hot meadow tea or a cold drink?"

They both said they would like a cold drink, so Nettie soon returned with three glasses of cold, sweetened garden tea and some chocolate whoopie pies, which she set in front of them.

Nettie nervously sipped her cold drink and looked at the bishop over the rim of her glass. Her eyes traveled upwards to the ceiling, where, to Nettie's dismay, she thought she could see fly marks. *I must clean the ceilings*, she thought. Nettie felt as if she were about to have a panic attack; her heart raced so loudly that she was sure the bishop and his *fraa* would hear it, and her mouth went dry. She stood up abruptly to hold out the plate of whoopie pies to them, hoping the action would somehow snap her out of the panic attack. However, as she did so, her wrist twisted and the pies flew off the plate. Mrs. Beiler leaped to her feet and helped Nettie scoop up the pies.

"I'll be right back," Nettie mumbled as she hurried out of the room. Once in the safety of the kitchen, Nettie threw the pies in the trash and hurriedly looked around for something to replace them. She took out a fresh plate, and heaped it up with several cinnamon bread muffins. Nettie took two, big, deep breaths, and then holding the plate tightly with both hands, made her way back into the living room.

Linda Beiler smiled warmly at her, which put her somewhat at ease. Nettie carefully offered them both a muffin, and then sat down with relief.

"How are you doing now, Nettie, without your *mudder*?"

The bishop's voice was kindly, and Nettie studied him for a moment. His *baard* was ginger and graying on the edges, and he had a long, narrow face, and a long nose. It was a face that reminded her of the face of Jebediah Sprinkler. Nettie shivered involuntarily. "I'm okay, *denki*," Nettie said.

"Do you feel you are ready to come to the church meetings now?"

"*Jah*," Nettie said, but then thought, *I actually don't know if I am ready for a crowd of people yet.*

The bishop continued his questions. "Do you have everything you need?"

Nettie nodded. "*Jah, denki*."

"I believe your *mudder* left the *haus* and farm to you, but all her money to a stray cat protection league."

Nettie shot a look at the bishop; how did he know? Who had she told? She bit her lip. "That's correct. I'm going to lease the land to the Glicks when probate is through, but as my lawyer told me that probate can take quite some time, I've found part time work with the Glicks."

Nettie noticed that the bishop and his wife exchanged glances and smiled at each other.

"That is *gut*," the bishop said. "Yet are you troubled, Nettie? You seem troubled about something."

Nettie sighed. *I should tell the bishop, I suppose*, she thought. Aloud she said, "I *am* troubled. A *mann* called Jebediah Sprinkler came to see me and said that my *mudder* made a new will leaving everything to him. He doesn't have a copy of the will and said that there's likely a copy somewhere here, in the *haus*."

The bishop nodded. "Ah, *jah*, I remember. Your *mudder* wanted you to marry the *mann* several years ago."

Nettie was taken aback, but then realized that of course the bishop would know about her brief and unwilling engagement to Jebediah Sprinkler. Back then, her *mudder* was not so much of a recluse. Nettie wondered who else in the community knew.

"And you have found no such will?" the bishop asked.

Nettie shook her head. "*Nee*, and I've spent a lot of time looking for it. If there is such a will, then I'll be homeless."

Linda Beiler spoke up. "*Nee*, Nettie, you mustn't think that. There would be a *familye* who would be happy to have you stay with them until you are married."

"Married?" Nettie was a little embarrassed that the word came out as a shriek, but why on earth would Linda Beiler mention marriage?

Linda smiled again. "Of course you will be married one day, Nettie." She would have said more, but the bishop interrupted her.

"Nettie, are you concerned about this *mann* taking away your *haus* and farm?"

"*Jah*."

The bishop smiled patiently, and said one word, "*Gelassenheit*."

"*Gelassenheit*?" Nettie repeated.

"Do you know that that means, Nettie?" The bishop's voice was gentle and kind.

"*Jah*. It means to submit; my *mudder* always said it."

The bishop smiled again. "It means to submit to the will of *Gott*," he continued, "even if it makes no sense to us. The ways of *Gott* are not the ways of man; who knows why *Gott* does what He does? But do you have faith that *Gott* will provide for you?"

Nettie wanted to lie and say, "*Jah*," but she did not in fact have faith that *Gott* would provide for her, which was precisely why she intended to destroy the will, if she found it. Yet she could not lie to the bishop. "I don't think I do have faith," she said slowly. "I do not want to be living with another *familye* when this is my own *haus* and farm. It's not fair." Nettie looked at the bishop to see how he was taking her disclosure.

He appeared unconcerned. "Do you remember when you were at *skul*?"

"*Jah*," Nettie said, puzzled.

"There was a little rhyme you said at *skul*, that all *kinner* say when they are at *skul*:

I must be a Christian child,

Gentle, patient, meek, and mild,

Must be honest, simple, true,

I must cheerfully obey, Giving up my will and way.

"Do you remember it?"

Nettie did remember the rhyme, but before she could say that she did, the bishop continued. "Nettie, you must give up your will and way. You must give up your will and way to *Gott*. It is the will of *Gott* that counts, not your will. You need to have faith that *Gott* will provide for you. Can you have that faith, Nettie?"

"I will try," Nettie said truthfully.

Chapter Eleven

Nettie woke up an hour earlier than her usual time. She tossed and turned, unable to get back to sleep. The bishop's words were still ringing in her ears. Sure, it was the right thing to do to surrender her will to *Gott* and have faith that He would provide for her, but what if *Gott* wanted her to be homeless and go live with a *familye*? She didn't think she could cope with that. Then again, she realized that not trusting *Gott*, even if He did want her to live with a strange *familye*, was showing a lack of faith and was not submitting to *Gott's* will.

Nettie pulled the quilt over her head, but her thoughts were still swirling around in circles, around and around in her head. Finally, she threw the quilt aside in disgust and got out of her bed. She made her way to the bathroom stealthily, until she remembered that her *mudder* had gone to be with *Gott*. Her *mudder* used to yell at her to bring her breakfast the second she heard Nettie awake.

Nettie stretched and yawned, and then hurried to the kitchen, with *kaffi* on her mind. She sat down and looked up at the old, oak mantle clock, an engagement gift from her *vadder* to her *mudder*. It was sitting in the kitchen, on a little wooden bench. It used to strike loudly every half hour, but Nettie stopped the clock after her *mudder* died. The noise had always grated on her, as had its loud tick-tock. Still, there was another clock in the living room, a much quieter clock.

Nettie shook her head and attended to the *kaffi*. Soon she was sitting back down with a mug of hot *kaffi* in her hands. Nettie took a sip and smiled.

As the sun was already up, Nettie walked outside to feed the chickens, but to her dismay, noticed at once that Blessing was in the herb garden. He had his head down, munching away. She was sure she had secured his gate properly, and her retired horse, Harry, was still in the field, grazing.

Nettie sighed. After scolding an indifferent Blessing for being a naughty boy and opening two gates, she led him back to the field and made sure the gate was securely latched, and then returned to the herb garden to inspect the damage.

Most of the herbs were untouched, but Blessing had eaten all the sage and the basil. Nettie used both herbs heavily. She used sage tea for sore throats and coughs as well as stomach upsets, and used to wrap her *mudder's* ankles in it when they swelled. Her *mudder* had also found a steam inhalation of sage helpful with her spring allergies. Nettie also used sage in cooking, in chicken casseroles, in meatloaf, and in stuffing.

As for the basil, Nettie was fond of using it too, especially in pesto, which was a favorite of hers. It was also wonderful in salads. Apart from cooking, Nettie used basil medicinally. Basil tea was excellent for soothing indigestion, and the macerated leaves were soothing for insect bites and stings.

Blessing had eaten all the basil plants and sage bushes right down to ground level, and these were two herbs Nettie always liked to have on hand. There was only one thing she could do; she would have to drive to town that morning and buy new plants from the plant nursery. There was still money in the cookie jar basket, and by the time that ran out, she would be earning an income from gardening for the Glicks.

Later that morning, Nettie drove Blessing to town. It was the first time she had driven any horse but Harry to town, but Blessing was entirely unconcerned by the cars that passed too close. Soon Nettie relaxed and enjoyed herself. She drove past stately, old beeches, and when she drove past the stream, she admired the spectacular colors of the wildflowers: the pale pink fading to white of the mayflowers, the bright pink of the moccasin flower, the bell-shaped blue and purple of the columbine, and the pastel pinks and blues of the somewhat disturbingly-named liverleaf.

Nettie loved the fragrance of spring, when the air was filled with the pleasant aromas of lilacs and sweet spices.

Nettie soon arrived at the nursery where she had bought all her plants previously. It was run by Amish, and Nettie was comforted to hear the words of Pennsylvania Dutch spoken around her, mixed as they were with *Englisch* words. Rows and rows of colorful, flowering plants vanished into longer rows of shrubs and trees. The air was thick with the smell of manure, and the day was warmer than usual for spring.

Nettie was sorely tempted by all the pretty flowers, the spreading Solomon's seal with its bell-like flowers, the vivid blue cornflowers and gentians, big, bright dahlias, masses and masses of creeping phlox in shades from subtle pinks to deep purples, the large, showy flowers of the begonias in every color imaginable, and petunias in every manner of color and pattern. The dusky pink and delicate looking but sturdy hellebores were her favorite. Nettie stood for a moment simply to marvel at *Gott's* creation.

Suddenly the hair on the back of Nettie's neck stood up, and she swung around to see what had caused this feeling of disquiet. Was that Jebediah Sprinkler over by the tomato plants? She could not be sure, and whoever it was had ducked away quickly behind a group of *Englischer* ladies.

Nettie had felt eyes on her, but had chided herself that it had been her imagination; after all, she was used to solitude and isolation. Being in a crowd of people would be expected to make her somewhat uneasy. Yet, she had distinctly felt that someone was watching her.

Nettie paid for her purchases and then struggled to carry all the plants and the packets of seeds out to the buggy. By the time she was half way to the buggy, she felt she would drop them all so placed them on the ground for a rest.

"Here, let me help you with those."

Nettie spun around to look into the kindly, blue eyes of Daniel. "*Denki*, Daniel, that's very kind." Nettie was glad that the words had come out automatically without so much as a quiver in her voice, as her insides were shaking from seeing Daniel Glick. His proximity made her nervous. Well, the sight of him alone was enough to make her nervous.

Nettie licked her lips as her mouth had run dry. As Daniel took the one remaining plant she was holding from her, their hands brushed and Nettie felt as if she had just been plugged into a generator. She stole a glance at Daniel and saw a slow flush travel up his cheeks. She wondered if he'd felt it too.

As they walked over to the buggy, Blessing turned his head and stared long and hard at the plants. "No, you can't eat those, too," Nettie said. "You've done enough damage as it is."

Nettie turned to help Daniel put the plants into the buggy and saw he was looking amused. She instantly felt embarrassed for talking to the horse.

"What damage did he do?" Daniel asked causally.

"He got out of his field and also opened the gate into the herb garden. He ate all the sage as well as all the basil, and those are two plants that I particularly rely on," Nettie said. "Did he ever open gates at your farm?"

Daniel shook his head. "*Nee*, but I'm not surprised that he can."

"Why?"

Daniel smiled down on Nettie. "Oh, I don't think I've ever mentioned it. I found Blessing too. It was one day when *Daed* and I were removing an old fence on the far side of our farm. We didn't know there was barbed wire on the bottom. *Daed* reached in and pulled hard and the barbed wire ripped his arm above his glove, making it bleed badly. I tore a piece off my shirt and bound his arm tightly, and was going to run to the barn to call the *doktor*, but at that very moment, Blessing appeared. He was trotting down the road with his driving bridle on, and the reins dangling around his legs."

"Where did he come from?" Nettie was intrigued.

Daniel shrugged. "I have no idea. All I know is, I jumped on him and galloped off to the barn to call the *doktor*. You wouldn't think so from the sound of it, but it was a nasty wound. That's why I called him 'Blessing.'"

"And you never found his owner?"

"*Nee*. I called the police; I told the bishop who contacted other communities - nothing. We even put a notice in the *Die Botschaft*, but no one ever came forward."

Nettie scratched her bonnet. "How strange. He surely can't be an Amish horse then, if no one contacted you after reading the national Amish newspaper."

Daniel nodded in agreement. "That's what my *familye* and I thought. We figured he must be some sort of show horse, but it's very strange that no one's ever looked too hard for him."

Their conversation ceased then, and Nettie wondered how she could keep Daniel talking, in order to keep him there just a little while longer. She felt inexplicably happy when he was around.

Just as the silence stretched to the point of making Nettie uncomfortable, Daniel spoke. "Would you like me to have a look at your gates and make them more secure for you? You don't want Blessing escaping again."

"*Denki*, Daniel. *Denki*," Nettie said again, embarrassed that her cheeks were hot and, no doubt, her face was beet red.

Chapter Twelve

Nettie watched Daniel walk away. "He is so handsome and kind," she thought. She went to untie Blessing, but then had a sudden thought—she had not seen the packets of ashwagandha seeds when she and Daniel had placed the plants in her buggy. Nettie hurried to look in the buggy, but there were no packets of seeds anywhere to be seen. *I must have left them when I put everything on the ground for a rest*, she thought, shaking her head.

Nettie hurried back in the direction of the

nursery. She had never seen ashwagandha seeds sold locally before and had only one solitary ashwagandha plant growing. Ashwagandha tea had always had a calming effect on her *mudder*, far more so than chamomile tea, and besides, ashwagandha was also effective against colds, as well as being a pick me up for tiredness. If Nettie had a restless night, she would always get up and make ashwagandha tea, and then would be assured of a *gut* night's sleep. Nettie had been overjoyed to find the packets of seeds, but now had lost them.

To her great relief, Nettie found the packets of seeds lying on the ground not too far from the nursery. Thankfully no one else had taken them, although she couldn't have been away for long. She picked them up, but before she could even straighten back up, another male voice addressed her. "Nettie Swarey."

Jebediah Sprinkler! So she had seen him after all. Nettie started so violently that she almost fell forward. Jebediah's hand took her arm to steady her, but she snatched her arm away.

"You!" she snapped, folding her arms across her chest. *He looks like a snake waiting to strike*, she thought.

"*Hiya*, Nettie. Have you thought more about the will leaving everything to me?"

"*Nee.*" *Only that I've been looking for it. If I had found it, I would have burned it*, Nettie thought, glaring at Jebediah. He had ruined her perfectly good day.

Jebediah smirked at her. "You don't seem happy to see me."

"Why would I be?"

"Let me guess," Jebediah said in his grating voice. "You're not happy that your *mudder* left everything to me in her will."

"You'll have to prove that first." Nettie noted, with some satisfaction, that her words removed the sneer from Jebediah's face. "My lawyer doesn't know anything about it."

Jebediah simply shrugged one shoulder. "That's none of my concern. I have *my* lawyer currently looking into it."

Nettie caught her breath at his disclosure, and anxiously gnawed on a fingernail.

"There's a café here, at the plant nursery."

"So?" Nettie snapped rudely. Nettie's *mudder* had brought her up to be polite. The Amish were invariably polite, but Nettie's *mudder* had seen to it that Nettie was trained to surpass even the most normal standards of politeness. Yet Nettie felt no remorse for speaking to Jebediah so rudely. He would see her homeless, if he had his way. He wasn't the one to get up at least once in the middle of every night to empty her *mudder's* bedpan. He wasn't the one to be on the receiving end of verbal abuse year after year. He wasn't the one who had led a life of isolation to the extent of being afraid of people. Why, it was amazing that Nettie had come so far in recent times as not to be afraid to be out in public that very day. No, he'd had it easy, and now he was trying to steal her own *haus* and farm from her.

Nettie stomped her foot. "You will not steal my *haus* and farm from me!" Her voice came out louder than she had intended, and Nettie did feel a moment of embarrassment when an *Englischer* couple shot her a sidelong glance before moving away, but that soon passed.

"That's what I want to speak to you about."

Nettie eyed Jebediah suspiciously. His voice had gone from grating to soft. *Is he trying to turn on the charm?* she wondered.

Jebediah did not speak again, and finally Nettie could stand it no longer. "What do you mean?"

Jebediah smiled. "I have no wish to turn you

out of your *haus*, so I've had an idea which might be to our mutual benefit."

Nettie frowned. She had no idea what Jebediah could have in mind, although she was sure that whatever it was, that she would not like it.

"Come and have *kaffi* with me," he offered, "and I'll tell you all about it."

"You can tell me all about it here." Nettie had no wish to sit down to *kaffi* with his *mann*.

"*Nee.*" Jebediah shook his head. "Come and sit down. What harm could it do? My treat."

"*Nee*," Nettie said in turn. "I shall pay my own way, but *denki* for the offer." Despite her mistrust of Jebediah Sprinkler, Nettie was curious to hear what he had to say. And, although the will had not yet come to light, if there was any way he was considering relinquishing his claim on her land, she wanted to hear about it.

With a deep sigh, Nettie reluctantly followed Jebediah back inside the entrance of the plant nursery and then turned left around a corner to the café. To Nettie's relief, the little café was all but deserted. She had never, in all her life, eaten anywhere but at someone's *haus*, and in recent years, that *haus* had always been her own.

Nettie sat down on a black wicker chair and surveyed her surroundings. It was a pretty café; the floor was made of red brick pavers, and so many huge ferns hung from baskets that it was all but impossible to see the ceiling. The tablecloths alternated between olive green and pastel floral patterns.

Jebediah had walked away and was looking at a menu. He soon returned and sat down opposite Nettie. "I know you said you wished to pay, but I've already paid for you. I ordered you a hot Rooibos tea and a ham sandwich with chips and pickle."

"*Denki*," said Nettie through clenched teeth. She did not know the protocol in such situations, for she had been sheltered from having to observe social niceties, but she thought that since she had said she would pay for herself, then Jebediah surely should have permitted her to pay.

Nettie had planned to leave as soon as she heard what Jebediah had to say, but now she had to wait for her food to arrive and then eat it, all the while being forced to put up with Jebediah's company.

"What is your idea?" Nettie thought the direct approach was called for.

"My lawyer is looking into the missing will," Jebediah said slowly, "and when the will is found, and it will be found eventually, under the terms of the will, I will own everything."

Nettie shifted in her seat. "But you said you had an idea for me to keep my *haus* and farm."

Nettie was growing impatient; what was Jebediah up to?

Jebediah ducked his head and looked up at Nettie from under his eyelashes. “This is a little embarrassing, Nettie.”

Nettie frowned. Did he have an idea, or not? Or was he simply trying to irritate her? At that moment, the food arrived, and Jebediah tucked into it. Nettie sipped her tea and waited for him to continue, which was difficult, as he was trying her patience.

Much to Nettie’s frustration, Jebediah did not continue until he had eaten his hot dog. She debated whether or not to leave then and there, but her curiosity got the better of her. If there was a chance that Jebediah would forego his claim on her land, then she had to know.

Jebediah sat up straight. “It was your *mudder’s* wish for us to marry, Nettie.”

"Well, it wasn't *my* wish." As soon as the words were out, Nettie gasped her at her own rudeness.

Jebediah did not appear to be offended, and continued. "Nettie, I know you'll say *No* outright to this, but I would like you to think it over. I know you think I'm not a nice person, but I'm a *gut* person, really." He smiled at Nettie. "I'd like you to consider marrying me."

Nettie gasped. "Marry, marry you?" she stuttered.

"*Jah*, marry me. Think it over. That way, you won't lose your *haus* or farm; we'll both own them. You can continue to stay in your *haus*, and you won't have any money worries at all."

Nettie was too shocked to speak, so just stared at Jebediah.

"And you won't have to do a thing," he

continued. “I’ll work the farm, and you will just have to look after me and our *kinner*.”

Nettie felt sick to the stomach as soon as Jebediah said the word “*kinner*.” *I’d rather be homeless and lose my haus and farm than marry Jebediah*, she thought, but wisely kept that opinion to herself.

Daniel walked into the nursery looking at the list that his *mudder* had given him. As he looked up from the list, he thought he saw Nettie Swarey having lunch with a *mann*. *Don’t be silly. It can’t be her*, he scolded himself, but could not resist walking over in the direction of the café for a closer look.

Sure enough, there was Nettie sitting with a tall Amish *mann*. Daniel was surprised at his initial feelings of jealousy, but even from the distance, Daniel could see that Nettie was upset. Could this be the infamous Jebediah

Sprinkler, the *mann* who wanted Nettie's farm? He debated whether to go over to speak to her, to make sure she was all right, but then decided against it. It wasn't his place to be Nettie's guardian and protector—not yet, any way. Daniel was determined that, at some point, it would.

Chapter Thirteen

It had been several days since Jebediah Sprinkler had asked Nettie to marry him, but she shook her head and shuddered every time she thought of it. It had spurred her on to find the will. Consequently, the *haus* was in disarray as Nettie had searched most of it. She had pulled boxes out of old cupboards and had diligently searched through the contents, most of which comprised musty, old, yellowing papers.

To make matters worse, there had been no

sign of Daniel Glick, despite him offering to fix the gates to prevent Blessing escaping. Her *mudder* had always said, "*Menner*, they're no *gut* for anything," and she was beginning to think her *mudder* was right. Jebediah Sprinkler was trying to steal her *haus* and farm, and, worse still, wanted to marry her—Nettie shuddered again—and then there was Daniel Glick, who had offered to fix her gates, but since then had been conspicuous by his absence.

The Glicks had asked her to start her gardening duties the week after the next church meeting, and Nettie, despite being slightly annoyed with Daniel over his absence, could not wait to see him.

Nettie turned her attention back to the will. There was a high cupboard above the aged, propane gas powered refrigerator and it was part of an old, built in unit. Nettie dragged one of the wooden kitchen chairs over to the refrigerator, and stood on it. She opened the door and was met with a horrible, musty smell. *I bet this cupboard hasn't been opened in years*, Nettie thought. She for one had not opened it, and her *mudder* had not been able to stand on a chair for many years, so she most certainly had not opened it, either.

Nettie reached into the dark, musty cupboard and grasped for a cardboard box that was just out of her reach. She stood on her toes and reached for it, and finally was able to drag it toward her. At that moment, the chair collapsed.

Nettie fell heavily to the floor. *The chair just collapsed without warning*, Nettie thought with surprise. *It just gave way without so much as a creak*. Nettie grasped her right ankle which was beginning to hurt.

Just then there was a knock on the door. "*Hullo*, Nettie?"

Nettie tried to stand, but her foot gave way. She sat back down on the floor and called out, "Is that you, Melissa?"

"*Jah*, it's me," Melissa called back.

"Come in. I'm in the kitchen."

Melissa looked horrified to see Nettie sitting on the floor and hurried over to her. "Nettie, whatever happened; are you all right?"

Nettie nodded. "*Jah*, the chair just collapsed. I was standing on it to get to that cupboard." Nettie pointed behind her. "Oh dear, look at the mess." There were papers spread all over the floor. Nettie sent up a silent prayer of thanks to *Gott* that the heavy box had not fallen on her head.

"Can you stand?" Melissa tried to help Nettie to her feet.

"Ouch."

"Oh Nettie, I must drive you to the *doktor*."

"*Nee, nee*," Nettie said. "It's not broken. It doesn't hurt too much; it just won't take my weight. I'm sure it will be better soon."

Melissa bit her lip and looked at Nettie for a moment. "All right then, but come on, I'll help you over to a comfortable chair. You should elevate your foot and I'll put some ice on it."

"And I have some arnica cream in the kitchen in a mason jar," Nettie said, "if you wouldn't mind getting that. It's labeled. It'll stop the bruising."

Melissa left, but soon hurried back with ice wrapped in a towel and the mason jar of arnica cream. "I had a look at the chair. Three of the spindles under the chair have snapped. I wouldn't sit on any of those other chairs in the set; they look so old and I don't think they're safe. How old are they?"

Nettie thought for a moment. "I think they were *grossmammi's*. They could be sixty years old for all I know."

Melissa shook her head. "Seriously, I don't think you should sit on any of the chairs. If one broke like that, the others are likely to as well. Anyway, I'll make you some hot meadow tea with honey for the shock."

"Actually, Melissa, if it's not too much trouble, would you make me some bilberry tea please? It will help with the bruising too."

"Oh yes, I think I saw bilberry tea in one of the mason jars when I was looking for the arnica," Melissa said.

Nettie was filled with gratitude. "I don't know what I would have done if you hadn't come along; I would've had to crawl everywhere."

Melissa waved her thanks aside. "You're *wilkum*, truly."

Soon, Nettie and Melissa were sitting, drinking bilberry tea. "You know, it doesn't taste too bad," Melissa said. "It's like a bitter, weak blueberry drink."

"You didn't put honey in yours too?"

"*Nee*." Melissa looked down at her cup and

Nettie felt that perhaps something was troubling her.

"Is everything all right, Melissa?"

Melissa looked even more uncomfortable. "The other day, Daniel saw you having lunch with a *mann*."

Nettie nearly choked on her tea; it went down the wrong way. After a moment of coughing and spluttering, she said in an animated voice, "That was no *mann*! That was Jebediah Sprinkler!"

"The *mann* who's trying to take your *haus* and farm?"

Nettie nodded and took another sip of tea. "*Jah*."

Melissa frowned. "Well then, why did you have lunch with him?"

Nettie thought for a moment. "I know it seems silly, but I agreed to have lunch with him as he said he didn't want to take it all away from me and he had an idea how I could keep it." Melissa looked pleased, so Nettie hurried to explain. "*Nee*, it's not *gut* news at all. It turns out his idea was that we should get married."

"Married?" Melissa repeated. "And you're not considering it, are you?"

Nettie was horrified. "*Nee*, of course not." She shuddered. "Oh, Melissa, he seems so awful, and he said he's seeing a lawyer about the missing will."

Melissa shook her head. "That's just it, isn't it - the will is *missing*, and so as long as it's missing, there's nothing he can do. Is your lawyer worried?"

"He doesn't seem to be, but he did say that if the missing will was later than the one that's going through probate now, that Jebediah Sprinkler will get everything." Nettie looked at Melissa, expecting her to look exceedingly worried, but she simply shrugged.

"Well, if it's *Gott's* will, it's *Gott's* will."

Nettie was puzzled. "What do you mean, Melissa? If Jebediah Sprinkler gets my *haus* and land, then I'll have nothing. I'll be homeless."

"Not homeless surely. The bishop will find you a *familye* to live with. You could even come and live with us."

Nettie was growing more exasperated by the minute. "But it's *my* property, *my haus* and farm."

Melissa shrugged again. "You have to have faith, Nettie, faith to leave it all in the hands of *Gott*. If it turns out that the will is found, well that will be only because *Gott* wants it to be found. *Gott* might have another plan for you."

That's what you think, Nettie thought with

some resentment. *Of course Gott wouldn't want me to be homeless. If I find that will, I will burn it.*

"Anyway," Melissa continued, "you could marry my *bruder*, Daniel."

Nettie spluttered over her tea once more. "Daniel? Marry?"

Melissa laughed at Nettie's discomfort. "*Jah*, he likes you. He was jealous about seeing you with that *mann*."

Nettie's heart raced and her palms grew sweaty. "Did he say so?" She held her breath until Melissa answered.

Melissa chuckled. "*Nee*, but he didn't have to. He was jealous all right, and I know he likes you. He's never been interested in any *maidel* before. I know a lot about *menner*; you know where I work, don't you?"

Nettie tried to remember. "*Nee*, I don't think so; I only know that you work three days a week."

Melissa nodded. "*Jah*, I work for a matchmaking agency. I mostly do the paperwork, but all the *menner* who are on the agency's books seem so predictable, at least on paper. I don't interview anyone. My boss Harriet does that. I'll never get married."

Nettie was so shocked that she forgot about her own predicament for the moment. "You'll never get married? What about *kinner*? Don't you want *bopplin*?"

"I do want *bopplin*," Melissa said, "but I don't want to get married until I'm almost too old to have *bopplin*." She chuckled.

The girls then sipped their tea in companionable silence. Nettie's thoughts soon drifted to Daniel. His *schweschder*, Melissa, had just told her that Daniel liked her. Nettie was also developing feelings for Daniel. Nettie saw a problem with this. If she destroyed the will, then she could not see herself courting Daniel at any time. Nettie would not be able to keep the fact that she had destroyed the will from Daniel, so then what sort of person would he think she was? As far as Nettie saw it, she had two choices if the will did come to light. The first was to destroy the will, keep her *haus* and farm, and deny her attraction to Daniel. The second was to let Jebediah Sprinkler have her own property, and throw herself onto the will of *Gott*.

It was only later that night, as Nettie tossed and turned in bed thinking over both options, that she thought that perhaps she should stop plotting and planning, and have faith to let *Gott* have His will and way in the matter.

Chapter Fourteen

Nettie drove Blessing to the Schlabachs' *haus* where the fortnightly church meeting was to be held on this occasion. She was in plenty of time, for the service always started at eight. Yet Nettie felt sick to the stomach with the thought of being around so many people. Sure, she had been around a crowd of people at the viewing and the funeral, but she was in such a state back then that she had paid it no mind. Now, however, she was actively dreading it.

Nettie tied up Blessing and was nervously making her way to the *haus*, when she heard a horse snorting. She turned around and saw that Blessing was walking away from the *haus*, pulling the empty buggy behind him. Nettie hurried after him and to her embarrassment, saw he had stopped next to the Glicks' *familye* buggy. The only Glick in sight was Daniel, who had just caught Blessing.

"Missing a horse?" Daniel asked with a twinkle in his eye.

"Oh, I'm so sorry, Daniel," Nettie said. "I know that I tied him properly. Perhaps he can undo knots as well as gates."

Daniel hung his head and avoided Nettie's gaze. "I must explain about not coming to fix your gates," Daniel said.

Nettie hurried to reassure him. "Oh, that's fine. I know you're very busy."

"It's not that," Daniel said, and a slow, red

flush colored his cheeks. "It's just that I didn't want to interrupt you if you had, *err*, guests."

"Guests?" said Nettie, being entirely perplexed.

Daniel turned to his horse and fiddled with its harness. "That day at the plant nursery, when I went inside on an errand for my *mudder*," he said over his shoulder, "I saw you having lunch with a *mann*."

Nettie was concerned. Surely Melissa had told Daniel? Or was he just checking for himself? "*Nee*, that was Jebediah Sprinkler, the *mann* who would like to steal my land. He said he had an idea how I could keep the land, and refused to tell me unless I had lunch with him. He asked me to marry him; his idea for me to keep the land was to marry him."

Nettie noted that Daniel, who had turned back to her and was gazing at her, looked annoyed but not surprised, so she figured that Melissa had told him after all. A little thrill of excitement ran through her as she realized that Daniel was indeed jealous. Suddenly, the sky looked bluer, the sun shone brighter, and she could hear birds happily singing. Nettie giggled as she wondered what had come over her.

"Obviously you refused." Daniel said it as a statement, not a question, but Nettie answered anyway.

"*Jah*, of course."

Daniel beamed. "Well, let me tie up Blessing next to my horse. Perhaps Blessing misses him." He ignored the fact that his horse did not seem quite so pleased in turn to see Blessing, as he squealed at him and struck at him with his hoof.

Nettie's stomach clenched, hoping that Daniel had made the suggestion in order to see her again after the church meeting.

Daniel and Nettie walked over to the

Schlabachs' *haus*, and Nettie was glad of his presence. She was now less afraid of going into the crowd of people and less dreading the curious looks that she knew were to come.

To Nettie's relief, Melissa was waiting for her just inside, in the room where the women were already seated on the backless, wooden benches. As the Schlabachs' *haus* was not as large as some, and certainly not as large as the some *familyes'* barns where the church meetings were often held in their turn, the *menner* were seated in an adjoining room. Nettie remembered the church services from the time before her *mudder* had become a recluse, and remembered that the ministers would walk between rooms while sharing *Gott's* word.

The women did look at her with curiosity, but their smiles held warmth and acceptance. Nettie was at once overwhelmed with a sense of community and caring.

The first song of the church meeting was, as always, from the Amish hymnal, the *Ausbund*. And, as always, the hymns were sung without music, and were sung exceedingly slowly. Nettie had not been to church for many years, and although she struggled for a moment with the first line of the song, *O Gott, Vadder, wir loben dich, und deine Güte preisen wir*, the words came back to her readily:

O God, Father, we praise you

And your goodness we exalt,

Which you, O Lord so graciously

Have manifested to us anew,

And have brought us together, Lord,

To admonish us through Your Word,

Grant us grace to this.

Open the mouth, Lord, of your servants,

Moreover grant them wisdom

That they might rightly speak your word,

Which ministers to a godly life

And is useful to your glory,

Give us hunger for such nourishment,

That is our desire.

Give our hearts understanding as well

Enlightenment here on earth,

That your word be engrained in us,

That we may become godly

And live in righteousness,

Heeding Your Word at all times,

So man remains undeceived.

Yours, O Lord, is the kingdom alone,

And the power altogether.

We praise you in the assembly,

Giving thanks to your name,

And beseech you from the depths of our hearts

That you would be with us at this hour

Through Jesus Christ, Amen.

Nettie knew that sixty five of the one hundred and forty songs of the *Ausbund* were composed between 1535 and 1540 by Anabaptists imprisoned in the dungeon of Passau Castle in Germany. Most of these men were awaiting the death sentence, and were later martyred. Nettie felt a sharp pang of conviction that these men were fully prepared to die for their faith, and by comparison, her own problems were completely inconsequential. What right did she have to go against the will of *Gott*?

The people had begun singing the second song, *Das Loblied.* This was always the second hymn sung at Amish church meetings.

My God, Thee will I praise

When my last hour shall come,

And then my voice I'll raise

Within the heavenly home.

O Lord, most merciful and kind,

Now strengthen my weak faith,

And give me peace of mind.

To Thee, in every deed,

My spirit I commend,

Help me in all my need,

And let me ne'er offend.

Give to my flesh Thy strength

That I with Thee may stand,

A conqueror at length.

Tears pricked at Nettie's eyes. The *Ausbund* hymns did reflect loneliness, sorrow and despair, but throughout all, they reflected that one should pour out one's troubles to *Gott*. These men, who suffered in the first great persecution of the Anabaptists, found reasons to praise and thank *Gott*, so who was Nettie to go against *Gott's* will?

The first sermon of the day lasted thirty minutes, and the subject was on leading a right life in the sight of *Gott*. Nettie was overwhelmed with guilt. If she destroyed the will, she would be doing the wrong thing.

By the time more Scriptures were read, and Nettie kneeled for the silent prayer before the main sermon, she had all but made up her mind what to do, should she find the will.

Chapter Fifteen

After the church meeting was over, Nettie walked outside into the spring air with Melissa, who introduced her to the other young women of the community. Some Nettie remembered from her days at *skul*, others she did not.

Nettie kept one eye out for Daniel, and could see him talking to some young *menner*. One *mann* she did see in another group caused her quite a shock. "Melissa," she whispered.

"Look, over there, see that *mann*? That's Jebediah Sprinkler."

"That's him?" Melissa looked long and hard at Jebediah before speaking. "I've seen him at church meetings before, but only recently. He's not from our community."

"*Nee,*" Nettie said in a low tone. "He's told me that he's staying with the Glock *familye*. He's only hanging around until the will is all sorted out." Just then, Daniel looked up at her and smiled, and she smiled back, before Daniel hurried away with other *menner* to convert some of the backless benches to tables for the meal.

Nettie and Melissa walked down to look at the Schlabachs' herb garden, and before Nettie knew it, it was the *youngie's* turn for the meal. Nettie followed Melissa back inside to the room where the young women were to eat. They ate in a separate room to the young *menner*.

Nettie sat down next to Melissa and looked at the cup, saucer, glass of water, and knife set at each place. In front of her was a veritable feast set on the table. Nettie fondly remembered from long ago the church spread, the combination of peanut butter, marshmallow crème, and corn syrup. Her *mudder*, unlike Nettie, did not have a sweet tooth, and would not allow Nettie to make anything that Nettie considered delicious.

Spread on the table along with *kaffi* and meadow tea, were snitz pies, cheeses, red beets, pickles, bread, jam, and apple butter. The menu for the meal following the church meeting was always the same, so that a *familye* could not become prideful by having different, possibly better, food than another *familye*.

As soon as the silent prayer before eating was over, Nettie spread some church spread on a piece of bread, while keeping an ear on the conversation. Up until now, the conversation had been about *bopplin* and about which young *mann* the girls were interested in, so Nettie pricked up her ears at the mention of Jebediah Sprinkler.

"Poor Lydia," a girl was saying. "She was heartbroken when Jebediah broke off their engagement. She thought everything had been going well too, so it came as a shock."

"Did he give her any reason?" the girl sitting opposite asked.

"*Nee*," the first girl said. "*Nee*, not at all, but the strange thing was that within a few weeks, he'd left their community and come here."

Melissa was listening to the conversation too, and she asked, "He's staying with the Glock *familye*, isn't he?"

"*Nee*," the girl said. "He was for a short time, but he moved into the B&B down by the stream. He told my *bruder* that he was coming into some money soon."

"Perhaps he has another girl," the second girl said.

The first girl laughed. "*Jah*, and a wealthy one by the sound of it."

Melissa and Nettie exchanged glances. "Jebediah must be sure there's a will," Nettie whispered to Melissa, "for him to break off his engagement as soon as my *mudder* died and then come to this community. He can't have been bluffing about the will after all."

"I think you must be right," Melissa said. "He is certainly a sneaky one. Now Nettie, are you going to the singing tonight?"

Nettie shook her head. "I think I have to work my way back into crowds slowly," she said with a rueful laugh.

"I understand. I'd be the same in your position. Besides, I don't like singings. I never go."

Nettie was puzzled. "Why not?"

"It's all just matchmaking really, and I work for a matchmaking agency. It's all too much like work to me."

"Matchmaking?"

Melissa laughed. "*Jah*, only the single young women and the single young *menner* go to singings. It's obvious, isn't it?"

Nettie was not sure, so merely smiled and nodded.

"You don't need to worry about Daniel, though," Melissa said. "He never goes to singings."

Nettie frowned at the mention of Daniel, but said, "I thought all the *youngie* went to singings."

"I told you, only the ones looking to get married."

Nettie could not resist asking, "But surely Daniel wants to get married?"

Melissa simply smiled to herself.

As their sitting of the meal was now over, Melissa and Nettie walked outside together. "Are you going home now, Nettie?" Melissa asked.

"*Jah*, but I can't right now."

Melissa frowned. "Why ever not?"

"'Cause I want to avoid Jebediah Sprinkler, and he's over by the buggies." Nettie nodded her head in his direction.

Melissa turned around to look. "*Ach*, well let's go back down to the garden until he leaves. We can keep an eye on him from down there."

Nettie and Melissa went back down to the flower bed, talking happily. If it hadn't been for Jebediah Sprinkler and the thought of the will in his favor looming over her, Nettie would have been happy. It was a beautiful, late spring day. The sun was shining; the birds were singing, and the fragrance of the flower beds was invigorating.

"Look at the butterflies around the bee balm; aren't they pretty." Nettie pointed to the exotic blue and black striped butterflies encircling the deep red tubular flowers. "I'm not surprised that the Schlabachs grow bee balm," Melissa said, "as they're beekeepers. *Mamm* loves the honey she gets from them."

Nettie turned to say something to Melissa, but she was looking over her shoulder. "I've got to run, Nettie. I'll talk to you later."

Nettie turned to see what or who was responsible for Melissa's hasty departure, and saw Daniel coming her way. *How embarrassing*, she thought. *Melissa left so that I'd be alone with Daniel. I hope Daniel doesn't think it was my idea.*

Daniel walked over to her. "*Hiya*, Nettie. Did you enjoy the church meeting today?"

Nettie smiled up at him shyly. "*Jah*, it was *gut*, *gut* to be back in the community again."

Daniel simply smiled and turned back to the garden. "You must love gardens, Nettie. Are you looking forward to starting work in our garden this week?"

"*Jah*, I am." *And all the more so because I'll see you*, Nettie thought, and then was embarrassed as her cheeks grew warm. *I hope I'm not blushing*, she thought, so bent forward to smell the lilac bush.

When she stood upright, Daniel was holding out some stems of lilac to her. They had the prettiest flowers of deep purple, edged with white. "I don't think the Schlabachs will mind," Daniel said as he offered them to her.

As Daniel handed Nettie the flowers, he did not let go as soon as she took them, and his hand lingered on hers for a moment. Nettie's face flushed again as she realized that he did so deliberately. *He must like me*, she thought, her heart all but beating out of her chest.

Nettie did not know how to react, so unaccustomed was she to being around young *menner*, so said the first thing that came into her head. "I wanted to go home, but Jebediah Sprinkler is over by the buggies," she blurted. "I think he wants to speak to me, and I want to avoid him, so Melissa and I came to the garden to wait for him to leave." As soon as the words were out, Nettie was annoyed with herself for saying them.

Daniel looked in the direction of Jebediah, and Nettie could see he looked none too pleased. "Would you like me to escort you safely to your buggy?'

"*Denki*, that would be *gut*."

Nettie and Daniel walked to the buggies, Nettie still annoyed with herself for bringing her time with Daniel to an end. She did, however, enjoy the feeling of being protected by Daniel. It made her feel all warm and fuzzy inside.

When they approached Nettie's buggy, Daniel positioned himself between Jebediah and Nettie, and both of them simply nodded to Jebediah, who was watching them through narrowed eyes. Daniel helped Nettie into the buggy.

Nettie drove home, daydreaming about what it would be like to be Daniel's *fraa*. In fact, so engrossed was she in naming their future *kinner* and imagining their happy *familye* life together, that she would have missed the turn to her *haus*, but Blessing took himself there anyway.

Daniel watched Nettie drive away, feeling Jebediah Sprinkler's eyes on him the whole time. He turned around, and Jebediah walked over to him.

"*Gude nochmiddaag*. I believe you're Daniel Glick? I'm Jebediah Sprinkler."

"Good afternoon," Daniel said in return, and then added, "I've seen you around, of course."

"*Denki* for looking after Nettie."

Daniel narrowed his eyes. It was clear that Jebediah was trying to imply that he was courting Nettie. Daniel just crossed his arms and stared at Jebediah.

Jebediah appeared to be disappointed that Daniel did not respond. "I can't say too much, but we will soon be neighbors," Jebediah said, with a calculating look on his face.

"Really," was all Daniel said.

"*Jah*." Jebediah pushed on. "I can't say too much," he repeated, "but I am soon to be married to a neighbor of yours."

"Really," Daniel said again. "Well, if you will

excuse me, Jebediah, I must be getting back to my *familye*."

Daniel left, pleased that he had managed to hold his tongue and keep his opinions to himself. The nerve of the *mann*, trying to imply that he was going to marry Nettie. Well, no names had been mentioned of course, but the implication was clear.

Chapter Sixteen

After the meal, Nettie drove home. The fact that Jebediah Sprinkler had gone so far as to break off his engagement and come to the community soon after her *mudder* died, did seem to suggest that there actually was a will in his favor. Otherwise, surely he wouldn't have bothered to go to such lengths.

Nettie set herself afresh to searching the *haus*. She started with the floorboards, checking to see if any were loose and thus could have something hidden under them. By the time she had been through the whole *haus* and not discovered any loose floorboards at all, it was almost dark, and she had to lock up the chickens. Her back was aching horribly from all the stooping over.

Nettie came back inside after her evening chores, somewhat refreshed by the fresh air. Nettie made a heap of mashed potatoes and then made some beef gravy and ladled it out so that the potatoes looked more like a little island in the midst of a sea of gravy. She heated up some chicken pot pie to go with it. As Nettie sat down to her meal, she remembered that her *mudder* once told her that *Englischers* don't usually mix beef and chicken in the one meal. *I wonder what made me remember that?* Nettie thought, as she spooned some beef gravy and chicken pot pie into her mouth.

Nettie was also uncomfortable on the kitchen chairs she had brought in from the barn, as they were not as high as the other set, and she felt like a child sitting at a high table. She had taken all the old worn wooden kitchen chairs out to the barn to avoid any possible further injury, and had fetched another set of old chairs from the barn and dusted them thoroughly. These looked the same age, but while the previous chairs had weak-looking spindles, these were a most sturdy melamine with metal bases and legs. There appeared to be no parts that could break, unlike the ladderback wooden chairs, which had six weak-looking spindles under the seat. The only drawback of the metal and melamine chairs, apart from their lack of height, was that they were a most glaring salmon-pink color. "At least they're safe," Nettie said aloud.

After that part of her meal, Nettie was still famished. She looked in the refrigerator, and saw the banana pudding. This was Nettie's own recipe—she always substituted half the sugar for maple syrup, so it was a delicious, gooey treat. Nettie helped herself to a big serving of the banana pudding. "I wonder why I'm so hungry tonight?" Nettie said aloud. "Oh, I know. *Mamm* always used to say that people get hungry when they're tired. I haven't had much sleep lately worrying about Jebediah Sprinkler and the will."

The thought of the will spurred Nettie into action. She washed the dishes and left them to dry on the rack, as was her habit. Her *mudder* had always said that drying dishes with a dish towel made germs grow, and her *mudder* had been obsessed with germs. Why she had so much clutter then, Nettie did not know.

"I wonder if there's still something up in that cupboard?" Nettie asked herself. She dragged one of the melamine and metal chairs over to the refrigerator, and then climbed on it. When she opened the cupboard above the refrigerator, Nettie realized just how much shorter these chairs indeed were. She got back down and looked around for something to extend her reach.

Nettie got the straw broom, and then climbed back on the chair. She poked the broom inside the cupboard, and found there was another box at the back of the cupboard, but, although the broom could prod it, she was unable to maneuver the broom to encourage the box to come out.

Nettie sighed and climbed down from the chair once again. She looked around the room, and her eyes alighted on the heavy, wooden, kitchen table. That would do; it was certainly high enough. The table proved to be harder to drag than it looked. It was of quarter sewn oak, and was quite a sturdy table. Nettie was relieved by the time she'd managed to drag it over to the refrigerator.

Nettie climbed up onto the table, and was able to see to the back of the cupboard. There was indeed a box, but old bits of yellowing, crochet lace were poking over the top. Nettie sighed with disappointment; she had hoped it would be a box of documents. Nettie dragged the box toward her and then placed it down on the table. She hopped off the table, and then sat on it to look through the box.

At first, Nettie picked up the crochet piece by piece, but then simply upended the box. There at the bottom, was an envelope. Nettie caught her breath. Even upside down, it looked important, for there was a deposit of what looked like candle wax on the back, sealing it.

Nettie picked up the envelope and stared at the back of it for a moment, before turning it over.

There, in her *mudder's* handwriting, was written:

The Last Will and Testament of Elma Swarey.

Chapter Seventeen

Nettie shook and shook. She carried the envelope into the living room and placed it on the little, round wooden table next to the big, blue sofa, and then sat down, staring at it.

This must be the will leaving everything to Jebediah Sprinkler. Was there any chance it was simply her *mudder's* copy of the previous will? There was a date next to the writing, but it had faded. Nettie peered at it until her eyes hurt, but could not make out the writing.

Nettie walked into her *mudder's* bedroom and

fetched the magnifying glass from beside her bed. Her *mudder* used to read the *Dordrecht Confession of Faith*, a booklet of statements of belief, including salvation by faith in Jesus Christ, baptism, and avoidance of violence, among others. It also included the *Martyr's Mirror*, the testimonies of Christian martyrs, most of whom were Anabaptists who were killed because of their belief in adult baptism, and the Bible in German, the Martin Luther version.

There was an oppressive atmosphere in her *mudder's* bedroom, and all the window-opening and spring cleaning since her *mudder* had died had not made much of an impression on it. Nettie hurried back out of the room.

She sat back down on the sofa and held the magnifying glass over the date. There was no doubt; the date was the very year that she had gotten engaged, against her will, to Jebediah.

There was only one conclusion to be had: the

envelope that Nettie was staring at was in fact the will leaving everything to Jebediah Sprinkler.

The next morning, Nettie got up just before the sun. She did not have many chores to do, but she had barely had a wink of sleep. Nettie walked to the living room to see if the envelope was still there. Yes, there it was. She hadn't dreamed it as she hoped she had.

Nettie rubbed her eyes and set to brewing the *kaffi*. With a loud sigh, she sat down to sip her *kaffi*. A headache was forming at her temples and she tried to rub it away, to no avail. Nettie wasn't at all hungry, but forced herself to eat stewed crackers in warm milk. After that, she paced up and down the kitchen.

The sun was coming up, and Nettie peered out the window at it. It looked like a fine day. *Fine for that Jebediah Sprinkler*, Nettie thought with resentment. Then she saw her old horse, Harry, grazing with Blessing in the field.

A thought occurred to her as she looked at Blessing. He was technically homeless, as no one knew who owned him, yet hadn't *Gott* provided for him? Then Nettie's mind was drawn to the Scripture, Matthew chapter six, verse twenty six: "*Look at the birds of the air: they neither sow nor reap nor gather into barns, and yet your heavenly Father feeds them. Are you not of more value than they?*"

Nettie walked into the living room and took up the envelope in her hands. "This envelope holds my future," she said aloud. Then she thought of Blessing, and *Gott* providing for the birds. "*Nee*, it is *Gott* who holds my future," she said firmly to herself.

Three hours later, Nettie drove Blessing to the phone shanty and made an important call, and a further three hours after that, there was a knock on her door.

Nettie opened to the door to a stooped Mr. Koble standing on the porch. “Come in,” she said to her lawyer.

“I must say, I was surprised when you told me there was another will,” Mr. Koble said.

Nettie nodded. “I was surprised, too. As it’s sealed, I wanted you to open it.”

“You did the right thing,” Mr. Koble assured her. “It might remove legal complications later.”

Nettie showed Mr. Koble into the living room and he sank into the deep sofa. Nettie handed him the envelope, and he took out an old gold-rimmed tortoiseshell case and from it removed his glasses. With them safely perched on his nose, he broke open the seal.

Nettie sat on the adjoining sofa, holding her breath, hoping that the will would not leave everything to Jebediah Sprinkler. She watched Mr. Koble carefully as he read it, looking for a change of expression. There was none, although his bushy white eyebrows did go up and down at intervals.

"Interesting," he finally said.

Nettie wanted to scream with impatience. "What does it say? Does it leave everything to Jebediah Sprinkler?"

"Indeed it does," said Mr. Koble.

"The *haus*, the land?"

"Everything," Mr. Koble said. "There are no cats as beneficiaries in this will."

Nettie bit her lip.

"Just one thing," Mr. Koble said, with a twinkle in his eye. "Do you have any intention of marrying this Jebediah Sprinkler?"

"*Nee*!" Nettie all but shouted. "Absolutely not, Mr. Koble, I can assure you of that." She wondered why Mr. Koble had asked such a question.

Mr. Koble smiled. “Nettie, there is a condition on this will. Jebediah Sprinkler only has claim to your mother’s entire property should you marry him within one year of her death.”

Nettie could scarcely believe her ears. “Could you please repeat that, Mr. Koble?” After Mr. Koble repeated it, Nettie asked, “So Jebediah Sprinkler doesn’t get anything?”

“Nothing at all, unless you marry him.”

“There’s no chance of that,” Nettie said, “although I did see him at the plant nursery recently and he asked me to marry him.”

The lawyer’s eyebrows shot up. “Did he indeed!”

“So what happens now, Mr. Koble? Do I inform Jebediah that I’ve found the will?”

Mr. Koble shook his head. “I suspect that Mr. Sprinkler has his own copy of the will, which is why he asked you to marry him. Leave it to me. Do you know his address?”

Nettie shook her head. "I only know he's staying at the B&B that's down by the stream."

"I shall send that young man a stern legal letter," Mr. Koble said. "I doubt that he will ever contact you again, but should he do so, please call me at once and I will see to him."

Nettie beamed. "Thank you, Mr. Koble, thank you so much."

Chapter Eighteen

Nettie walked outside and watched Mr. Koble drive away in his expensive looking car. She remembered the last time that Mr. Koble had been here, that Blessing had appeared soon after Mr. Koble had left.

And now were her eyes deceiving her, or was this Blessing trotting down the road toward her?

I hope this isn't all a dream, Nettie thought, and then shook her head to clear it. She looked again, and sure enough, it was Blessing coming, only he was being driven by Daniel Glick.

"I just don't understand it," she said by way of greeting when Daniel approached. "I only drove Blessing to the phone shanty just a few hours ago. I didn't know he'd escaped again."

"*Hullo* to you too," Daniel said. "What a fine greeting that is." His manner was teasing, but Nettie still blushed.

"I'm sorry," she said. "*Hiya*, Daniel."

"*Hiya*, Nettie." Daniel laughed.

"I'm so sorry that Blessing escaped again."

"My fault entirely," Daniel said. "I never did come to fix the gates. I suppose you're wondering why I'm driving him."

"Yes, now that you mention it," Nettie said. *I hope Daniel isn't going to take Blessing back*, she thought. *He's my only means of independence.*

"I was going to come and see you today, and when Blessing turned up this morning, I thought I should drive him here and invite you for a buggy ride."

Nettie gasped and her hand flew to her mouth, then she chided herself for being so obvious. She stared at Daniel with her mouth open. *Buggy rides mean courting*, thought Nettie, her heart all at once going ninety to the dozen. Nettie did not know what to say, until she saw disappointment register on Daniel's face, so she thought she should hurry to reassure him.

"I'd love to," she said, in all too animated a fashion, and then remembered that her *mudder* had always said, "*Menner* will never respect you if they know that you like them," and, "You must never let a *mann* know that you like him or you'll make a fool of yourself."

Daniel's face lit up and Nettie's heart skipped a beat. "Is now a *gut* time for you?"

Nettie hesitated, only for a second, as she thought of her *mudder's* advice and words, but then decided to put it all behind her. She would not look to the sadness of the past, but would press onwards to the future that *Gott* had for her. "Yes, it's a *gut* time," she said.

Nettie climbed into the buggy, next to Daniel, and Blessing trotted happily down the roads that wound their way between farms, with their pretty white barns and old white stone buildings that stood in contrast to the lush green of the fields. The gentle breeze blew in her face, and she stole a look at Daniel.

Daniel caught her eye and smiled. "I passed a car on my way to your *haus*."

"*Jah*, that was my lawyer. Oh Daniel, I forgot to tell you! I found the will."

Daniel sucked in a breath. "The will leaving everything to Jebediah Sprinkler?"

Nettie laughed. "*Jah*, but that's just it—it doesn't."

"It doesn't?" Daniel echoed.

"*Nee*," Nettie said. "Not exactly. He gets everything only if I marry him within twelve months of *Mamm* going to be with *Gott*."

Daniel slowed Blessing to a walk and looked over at Nettie. "And you don't intend to marry Jebediah Sprinkler?"

Nettie thought he was still teasing, but said, "*Nee*, of course not." She shuddered involuntarily.

"*Gut*," Daniel said, still looking at her. "I would be very upset if you married another *mann*."

Nettie's face burned and her ears grew hot. She smiled shyly and then looked away. Her stomach was churning. *Did he say what I think he just said?* she asked herself, and then, as if knowing her shyness, Daniel reached out and took her hand.

Nettie smiled as his strong hand wrapped around hers. She loved the feeling, even if it did make her feel slightly sick to the stomach and have the same effect as the time she had accidentally touched the neighbor's electric fence.

"Jebediah Sprinkler told me that the two of you were betrothed," Daniel said. "Well, he didn't actually mention your name," he added, "but the implication was quite clear."

Nettie wasn't surprised. She wouldn't put anything past the unscrupulous Jebediah Sprinkler. "He did? When?"

"Yesterday, after the church meeting."

"And you didn't believe him?"

"*Nee*." Daniel squeezed Nettie's hand. "Do you believe that *Gott* has the right *mann* for every woman and the right woman for every *mann*?"

"Why, yes, I do believe that," Nettie said, comfortable with the fact that such was the belief of all Amish.

"Nettie, the second I laid eyes on you, I knew you were the woman that *Gott* had for me."

Nettie blushed again. She could not believe that such great happiness was hers. Yet there was something niggling away at her. "Daniel, I must tell you that when I was sixteen, my *mudder* arranged me for to be betrothed to Jebediah Sprinkler."

Daniel looked shocked, but merely asked, "What happened?"

"I refused of course, and that was the end of it, although my *mudder* was very angry at the time. Well, I think she was always angry. She never forgave me for it, and she always used to mention him to me."

Daniel turned to smile at her again. "You did very well to stand up to your *mudder*."

Nettie sent up a silent prayer of thanks to *Gott* for Daniel being so understanding. Yet there was one more thing she had to tell him. "Daniel, I must tell you that I'm not a *gut* person. When Jebediah told me about the will, I thought I would destroy it."

Daniel simply chuckled.

"Seriously, Daniel, I really did consider burning it."

Daniel did not appear to be concerned. "When did you change your mind?"

"Yesterday, at the church meeting, although up until then, I really did think about destroying it." Nettie looked at Daniel to see how he was taking the news.

"Nettie, it doesn't matter that you thought that you might. The point is, that you didn't. That's all that counts. Everyone has struggles —we all have fallen short of the glory of *Gott*.

Yet, after your struggle, did you find greater faith?"

"Why yes, I did," Nettie said, thinking how wise Daniel was and glad that he did not think less of her for her struggle.

Daniel drew Blessing to a stop by the stream, and helped Nettie down from the buggy. "It's so beautiful here," he said, gesturing around him. "The fullness of *Gott's* creation."

Nettie had to agree, as they walked alongside the stream under a canopy of tulip poplars which were in full bloom, giving off a subtle yet sweet fragrance.

Daniel turned to her. "Nettie, I can't tell you how happy I am that we're courting now."

Nettie's face flushed with happiness at his words.

"And one day," Daniel continued, "when we know each other better, I will ask you a very important question, and I'm hoping you will say *yes*."

Of course I will, Nettie thought, elated, but she simply smiled up at him.

The two of them walked, hand in hand, down along the stream, beginning the first day of the rest of their lives together.

Next Book in This Series

THE AMISH BUGGY HORSE, BOOK 2

Hope

Melissa Glick is happy in her job filing paperwork for a matchmaking agency. When her boss becomes ill, Melissa must step into her shoes and interview clients. All goes smoothly until she meets the agency's most difficult client, the former Amish man, Victor Byler, who complains about every date she arranges for him. Her boss insists that Melissa go to dinner with Victor Byler to find out the source of his issues.

What is holding back Victor Byler from finding true love?

Can Melissa stop herself falling in love with this man who does not know what he wants, and worse still, is no longer Amish?

About Ruth Hartzler

USA Today best-selling author, Ruth Hartzler, was a college professor of Biblical history and ancient languages. Now she writes faith-based romances, cozy mysteries, and archeological adventures.

Ruth Hartzler is best known for her Amish romances, which were inspired by her Anabaptist upbringing. When Ruth is not writing, she spends her time walking her dog and baking cakes for her adult children, all of whom have food allergies. Ruth also enjoys correcting grammar on shop signs when nobody is looking.

www.ruthhartzler.com